GRASP THE THORN

LION'S ZOO
BOOK TWO

JUDE KNIGHT

TITCHFIELD
PRESS

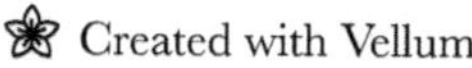 Created with Vellum

GRASP THE THORN

An accident brings them together. Will a scandal tear them apart?

Bear Gavenor has retired from war and built a business restoring abandoned country manors to sell to the newly rich. He'd like to settle in one himself and raise a family, but the marriage mart is full of harpies like his mother.

Rosa Neatham's war is just starting. Penniless and evicted from her home, she despairs of being able to care for her invalid father. When she returns to her former home to pick his favourite flower, she is injured in a fall.

Bear, the new occupant of the cottage, offers shelter to her and her father. When scandal erupts, he offers more. He wants a family. She needs a protector. A marriage of convenience will suit them both, and perhaps grow to be more.

When secrets, self-doubts, and old feuds threaten to destroy their budding relationship, can they grasp the thorn of scandal to gather the rose of love?

GRASP THE THORN WAS FIRST
PUBLISHED AS HOUSE OF
THORNS.

The story in this book was first published as *House of Thorns*. If you read that book, you may recognise the names of the characters and the plot. I've rewritten and polished, and changed details needed to bring the story into line with the rest of the series.

CHAPTER 1

Wirral Peninsula, Cheshire, 1816

The intruder stealing his roses had delectable ankles.

Bear Gavenor paused at the corner of the house, the better to enjoy the sight. The scraping of wood on stone had drawn him from the warmth of the kitchen, where the only fire in this overgrown cottage kept the unseasonable chill at bay. He had placed each foot carefully and silently, not from planned stealth, but from old habit. The woman perched precariously on the rickety ladder seemed oblivious to his presence.

Or—his sour experiences as a wealthy war hero in London suggested—she knew full well, and her display was for his benefit. Certainly, the sight was having an effect. Her skirt rose as she stretched, showing worn but neat walking shoes. Her inadequate jacket moulded to curves that dried his mouth. Wind plastered her skirts to lower curves that had him hardening in an instant, visions of plunder screaming into his mind.

It had been too long since his last willing widow.

Disgust at his own weakness as much as irritation at the invasion of his privacy, fuelled Bear's full-throated roar, "Who the hell are you, and what are you doing with my roses?"

She jerked around, then cried out as the rung she stood on snapped free of the upright. Bear lunged toward her as the ladder slid sideways. One upright caught on the tangle of rose branches and the other continued its descent. The woman threw out both hands but the branch she grasped snapped free and—before Bear could throw himself under her—she crashed onto the ground.

If the fall was deliberate—which would not surprise him after some of the things women had done to attract his attention—she had made too good a job of it. She lay still and white in a crumpled heap, her head lying on a corner of a flagstone in the path. He dropped to one knee beside her and slipped a hand into the rich chestnut hair. His fingers came away bloody.

He ran his hands swiftly over the rest of her body, checking for anything that seemed twisted out of shape or that hurt enough to rouse her. She had some scratches and a couple of puncture wounds in her hands. He removed one of the culprits—a large thorn snapped from the branch that failed to break her fall. Vicious thing, that rose, but the wounds it left were not life-threatening.

A large drop of rain splashed onto his neck, followed by a spattering of more and then a deluge. He cursed as he lifted the woman and ran into the house through the garden doors that opened from the room he'd chosen for his study.

She was a bare handful, lighter than she should have been for her height, though well-endowed in all the right places. He set her on the sofa and straightened. He needed a doctor.

The drumming of rain on the flagstones suggested neither of them would be going anywhere for a while. Bear couldn't take her out in this weather, nor could he leave her alone in the empty house.

Pelman, the local agent for the man who had sold him the house he was here to restore and sell, had been asked to hire servants, but had been full of excuses. "People won't come the distance from the village just for the day," Pelman had said.

As a consequence, he had an unconscious woman depending on him for her care, and—if Pelman was to be believed—no one else for at least a mile all around. By which the man meant no gentry, presumably, for he'd seen some farm cottages.

Perhaps she was from one of them? If so, she was a servant, and a poorly paid one, at that. She was in near rags, neatly mended and clean, but much washed and threadbare. The shoes displayed by his careless disposition of her skirts were likewise clean and polished, but worn to holes in the sole.

Step one. Clean the wound so he could see how bad it was.

He found a bowl on a shelf in the kitchen and poured lukewarm water from the kettle into it. He'd been here only long enough to assemble a stew for his supper, which hadn't begun to boil, and to glance into each room to figure out what space he had available.

The pantry boasted a row of neatly marked jars filled with herbs. Chamomile. That was good for healing. Yes, and here was a pottery tub of calendula paste. A basket on the floor yielded neat squares of linen. An old sheet, perhaps? Washed so thin that the remnants were fit only to be used as cleaning rags.

She was still unconscious when he returned to the room, her chest rising and falling as she breathed. He put the bowl on a small table near the sofa. With a bit of manoeuvring, he managed to drape the lady sideways so he could sit on the edge of the couch and reach the wound on the back of her head.

He dabbed gently at the blood.

Pelman had said Bear would need to resign himself to having servants sleep over. Pelman's sister was willing to serve as Bear's housekeeper, starting immediately, if she were permitted to sleep at the cottage. Bear had not met the lady, but was wary of allowing a female under his roof except in the company of others.

His huff of laughter lacked amusement. Despite his rejection of Miss Pelman, he had an unknown female on his hands, and his manservant was not due for several more days, since Jeffries travelled at a speed that avoided strain on Bear's horses.

Could the woman be Pelman's sister, come to secure her position? On the whole, he thought not. She looked nothing like the fleshy steward with his receding, dirty-blond hair. Besides, Pelman dressed in the height of fashion, so would surely dress his sister better than this.

His dabbing had started a seep again, but at least he could now see the wound properly. Said female had quite an egg, which had split and bled into her wealth of rich chestnut hair.

She groaned, then suddenly surged away from him to the back of the couch, twisting to shove him as hard as she could.

CHAPTER 2

A trespasser sat in her little sitting room, and her head hurt. As she slowly regained her wits, Rosabel Neatham shrank against the back of her couch and pushed at the giant who hovered over her.

The giant leapt to his feet and took a step back, his light blue eyes fixed on hers, his thick blond brows drawn together in a glower.

"Get out of my house," she said, without conviction. Some memory tried to break through the headache. Something to do with Pelman, that horrid man.

"*You* are in *my* house," said the giant, looking down his long nose at her.

The memory clarified, making her wince. He was right. Pelman had thrown her and her father out of Rose Cottage, citing instructions of the new owner. Pelman had found them another place; a shack that kept out most of the wind and the rain. He said he could find them something pleasanter if Rosa could afford to pay. One way or another.

The giant must be the new owner, who had bought Thorne Hall and all its farms and cottages, including Rose Cottage, from the nephew of the old baron. The most popular topic of conversation in the village for weeks was what he planned to do with Thorne Hall, with its fire damage and its collapsed wing. "You are not meant to be here yet," she said. Not her most brilliant remark, but her head felt ready to split in two.

The giant cast his eyes up to the ceiling, as if offering a prayer. Or, more likely, a complaint to some heavenly arbiter of unoriginal comments.

Outside the open doors to the terrace, a bright flash of lightning was followed almost immediately by a rolling peal of thunder. She winced at the noise. Father would be frightened. Since his mind had started to fail, storms disturbed him. Until the accident that confined him to bed, she had to watch him carefully to stop him from wandering into the storm, looking for something he could not articulate.

"I have to go," she told the giant, but when she put her feet on the floor and tried to stand, the right foot collapsed under her. A stabbing pain made the room swim before her.

The giant caught her before she fell and lowered her to the couch, swinging her feet up and pushing her back onto the cushions. "Is it your head?" he asked.

"My ankle." With her head and ankle both supported, the pain reduced enough for thought, but she still couldn't remember the giant's name.

He stood, looking down at her shod foot, his mouth twisted, his brows drawn together and his eyes sombre.

"I need to go home," she insisted. "My father is confined to bed, and he will be worried." Not about her, whom he didn't recognize, but certainly about the storm and about being alone. He had been asleep when she ventured out, but he never slept for long, and she should have been home long since—in the nasty little shack that was all the home she could afford.

"I think, Miss Whoever You Are, that you need to resign your-self to waiting out the storm," the giant said, his tone cold. "May I suggest that, on future occasions, you remain with your father instead of going off on your own to steal someone else's roses?"

Rosa flushed. They were his roses. She knew that quite well.

However, Father had been asking for roses for two days. When someone in the village mentioned that the rambler at Rose Cottage had flowered even in this cold and blustery weather, so unlike any summer in living memory, she had seen the opportunity to bring him the comfort of the flower he loved.

Rosa sighed. "I am Rosabel Neatham. And I apologize about the roses. I did not know you had arrived yet, Mr...."

The thick brows lifted, conveying suspicion with an edge of laboured patience, but he responded, "Gavenor. At your service, apparently. May I examine your ankle, Miss Neatham? It is Miss Neatham?"

She coloured again, the hot blood flooding her cheeks. Yes, it was Miss Neatham, though she was in her thirties. No one had ever seriously courted her, except the loathsome Pelman. Rosa had soon discerned that the arrangement he wanted fell short of marriage. Not that she would consider him as a husband if he offered.

"Miss," she confirmed. "Is it... Do you think you need to? I am sure..."

"I am sure you cannot stand on it, Miss Neatham, and someone needs to check that it is not broken. I can do it, or you can do it, for there is no one else in the house." His bored expression and voice were unaccountably reassuring. Pelman would be salivating at the thought of her baring her stockinged foot. The giant—Mr Gavenor—looked as if he would rather eat poisoned rat bait.

Rosa nibbled her upper lip while she thought, but really, she had no choice.

"Very well," she conceded. Then, since that seemed decidedly ungracious and one of them should show some manners, she added, "Thank you, Mr Gavenor."

The fairy would be white with pain if her embarrassment hadn't turned her a deep rose pink. Bear rather enjoyed discomforting her; a small revenge for his own awkwardness. He could manage the ladies of Society well enough. Harpies, the lot of them. He knew what they wanted and was not interested in giving it to them. The wives of his business acquaintances wanted little from him except attention to their husbands, which suited him nicely. Blushing fairies were a new experience, especially one with a determined chin who spat at him like an angry kitten and did not back down when he growled.

He knelt on the floor by her feet and examined her ankle. The flesh was swollen and held the indentation when he pressed it with his finger. Broken? Or sprained? He palpated and moved it, watching her face for a reaction. She managed not to make a sound, but the colour had receded from her face altogether, and sweat stood out on her white face. She lay against the pillows, biting her upper lip.

"Not broken, I think," he said at last. "But you have a bad sprain, Miss Neatham. You will not be standing on this foot for some time."

Miss Neatham's forehead creased in a frown. "But I must go home," she repeated, as if wishing would make it so. Undoubtedly, such a beauty had more than her share of courtiers falling over themselves to make her wishes come true.

He didn't bother with her nonsense. "May I remove your shoe to see if there is damage to the rest of the foot?"

She nodded, and Bear slipped her shoe off as gently as he could.

"The worst is over," he reassured her.

She managed a small twist of the lips that may have been a smile.

He was impressed by her attempt. He returned his attention to her foot, but the only problem appeared to be her ankle. "I do not see how you can go anywhere, Miss Neatham. You cannot walk on that ankle, and I have no carriage." Though, if he had one, he would send for a doctor. The ankle would heal with rest, but he could not be easy about the knock she had taken on her head.

"A horse?" she asked. "Could I borrow your horse?"

She had the grace to sound doubtful. *Borrow a man's horse, indeed.* Even if he had been inclined to put a beast of his into the keeping of a chance-met rose thief, he had no choice but to deny her. "Stabled in the village," he said. The shed here would not keep out the rain, and the stables at the Hall were in a worse state.

"Then a walking stick," she proposed. "I think there are some in the stand in the hall, unless Mr Pelman removed them."

Bear lifted his brows. "You know Pelman, then?"

"Everyone knows Mr Pelman," Miss Neatham's arid tone said more than her words.

He was unaccountably cheered that she did not admire the man, which made his response more abrupt than he intended. "You are being ridiculous, Miss Neatham. You can go nowhere in this weather and on that ankle, and you should not, in any case, be walking after such a blow to the head."

"But I must," she repeated. "Mr Gavenor, you do not understand. My father is bedridden and frail. I must go to him."

"Your servants will look after him."

The fairy shook her head. "I have no servants."

That was a conundrum, though he should have guessed it. Her accent belonged to the gentry, which had deceived him into forgetting about the evidence of her patched clothing and inadequate shoes. However, it begged the question of why the fairy had walked all the way to Rose Cottage, abandoning the poor man in his bed. In any case, he could not see what either of them could do about the situation.

"Resign yourself to remaining here until the rain stops, Miss Neatham. I will then walk into the village and arrange for transport. Meanwhile, surely one of the neighbours will call in and look after your father?"

Her look conveyed sheer disbelief. She hoisted herself upright, holding onto the side arm of the couch to balance herself on her good foot. "Unless you mean to keep me prisoner, Mr Gavenor, I am leaving," she proclaimed, her defiance diminished when she put the damaged appendage to the floor, turned even whiter and suddenly sat down. "Oh dear," she said.

Bear shook his head, sighing. "Give me your father's direction and I will see to him. You, Miss Neatham, sit here with your foot up until I return."

"There is a large umbrella in the stand, too," she told him, "and an oiled coat hanging on the back of the scullery door."

His face twisted into a suspicious scowl. "You are remarkably well informed about the contents of my house."

The woman showed no signs of fear at his expression or his tone. "I should be, Mr Gavenor. For the past eight years, until a week ago last Wednesday, Rose Cottage has been my home."

CHAPTER 3

As he trudged through the rain, Bear thought about Miss Neatham's claim. He couldn't imagine why she should make up such a story. She must know that he could check with Pelman. She did not seem a stupid woman.

His seller told him that the Hall was uninhabitable, but that a local fellow had been keeping an eye on the place and might know of a suitable cottage. He'd sent a letter to Pelman, asking for something close to the Hall. It had never occurred to him he might be turning a woman and her elderly father out of their home.

His instincts and the evidence said she was telling the truth. He found it hard to believe that a woman would want to live so far from the village.

On the other hand, everything was where she said it would be, down to the basket of ointments and potions for medical care in the pantry, to which he had been sent when he proposed tearing up a sheet to bind her ankle so she would be more comfortable. Sure enough, the basket held rolls of fabric, torn into two-inch strips and neatly rolled.

He'd wrapped the ankle and put the basket away, leaving her with a little jar of ointment to dab on her scratches. And that was another question. How did she come to leave the basket behind? If it was, indeed, hers?

He reached the bottom of the first hill and crossed a little bridge before climbing the next hill. In daylight, before the rain set in, the distance had seemed shorter.

Bear and Pelman had probably done Miss Neatham a favour, pushing her into a cottage within easy reach of the village shop and neighbours. He consoled himself with that thought as the rain poured down in sheets and the puddles joined into streams, running down the road and passing him as he descended a long slope toward a cluster of rooftops around a spire.

The village of Kettlesworth occupied a small plateau halfway down the hill, and spilled across the slope below to the river flats, now drenched in rain. The village boasted rows of tidy cottages as well as some shacks barely worthy of the name, and a number of larger buildings. The inn, where he'd eaten lunch today and left his horse, was centrally placed, where the road from the Mersey met four local roads, one of which led to the road to Chester.

Three other large buildings stood on their own extensive grounds. One, he knew, was occupied by the Pelmans, brother and sister. He'd called there this afternoon to collect the keys to the cottage from Pelman. A second building, beside the church, would almost certainly be the Rectory. The third large house stood slightly uphill from the village and faced the road he walked. Miss Neatham's directions led him past its gates and on past the first row of cottages. Fair enough. Her evident poverty made a large house unlikely. One of the cottages, then. At the crossroads with the inn, his instructions said to turn into the second road past that building. Ah. The road to the Pelmans' house. But no, she said to take a turn behind the church.

This lane was narrow and rutted. It wound down a hill too steep for carriages, lined by nothing much beyond rocks, goat shelters and pocket-handkerchief gardens, the last two drooping in the rain.

Soon, he arrived level with the roofs he had seen from the top of the road, and a miserable lot they were—more patch than roof and more hole than either. What idiot had thought it a good idea to build in a hollow? In this weather, the alley between the two-up two-down double row of dwellings was close to a lake, and the disgraceful condition of the cottages suggested they were either deserted or occupied by those who had no resources to do repairs.

Bear shook his head. He'd seen many such warts on the landscape; some landowner's idea of workers' housing, tucked into any corner—however unsuitable—that placed them out of sight of the local landowners and those visitors they wished to impress.

Miss Neatham could not possibly live here. Bear looked for a street name but found none. He tried the key she had given him in the door of the third house on the left. It fitted. What the hell was a lady of Miss Neatham's refinement doing in a slum like this?

Bear pushed the door open and let himself into a narrow hall, where he removed his coat and hat, and looked around a little helplessly for a hook or a rack or even a chair to lay them over. In the end, he draped the coat over the newel post of the staircase, and put the hat on the floor by the door. Puddles began to spread across the bare board beneath both. At least he wasn't destroying Miss Neatham's carpet.

Where would he find the father? He called out, "Mr Neatham?"

All he heard was the rain driving viciously against the outside of the house and his coat dripping on the floor.

Bedridden, she had said. Upstairs then. "Mr Neatham?" He repeated the call at the turn of the stairs, and again when he reached the landing.

"Who's there?" the voice from the room at the end of the short passage above the stairwell shook with fear or age, or perhaps both. "Who's there? Go away! I am armed. Rosie? Rosie, someone is in the house. Run, Rosie. Get the constable."

Bear pushed open the door to find an elderly man, not much larger than the rose thief herself, propped up on pillows in his bed, clutching a sheet to his chest, his eyes wide. He flourished a candlestick, his gaunt, wrinkled face showing more terror than aggression.

Bear stopped in the doorway. "Mr Neatham, your Rosie sent me."

Mr Neatham lifted his chin and sniffed. "I do not know you, sir."

The voice, thready with age, bore the same hallmarks of birth and education that distinguished his daughter's.

Bear bowed. "Allow me to introduce myself. Hugh Gavenor, at your service."

The room contained little beside the man and the bed. The corner of the bedside table rested on a stack of broken brick in lieu of a leg. A battered trunk and a few garments hanging on hooks along one wall completed the room's furnishings. The room was clean, almost painfully so, except the strong smell of fresh urine hinted that another clean—of the frail body before him—was overdue.

Neatham seemed to have forgotten his alarm in his puzzlement. "Gavenor? I know no Gavenors."

"I purchased Thorne Hall." Bear stepped toward the bed, stopped, and waited for Neatham to react to his approach.

The man curled his lip. "Rubbish. If you mean to tell me stories, Gavenor, or whatever your name is, you will have to do better than that. Lord Hurley would never sell. He would certainly never sell without telling me. I am his librarian, you know." He shook his finger at Bear. "Go off with you. My Rosie will be here soon with the constable."

Bear kept his countenance calm while he rehearsed a rebuke for Miss Neatham. *Your father is senile, woman. Why did you not tell me?*

"I came from your Rosie," he explained. How much could the old man understand? "She is at Rose Cottage. I am sorry to inform you she has injured her ankle and will not be able to return tonight. I came on her behalf, to check that you have all you need, Mr Neatham."

Neatham flapped his hands in agitation, almost hitting himself with the forgotten candlestick. "I don't believe you. I don't believe you. My wife Rosie would never stay at the gardener's cottage. Why should she? Lord Hurley will send some footmen to bring my wife home. I will…"

His wife? Bear shook his head to clear it. Miss Neatham's mother, presumably.

Mr Neatham stopped in mid flow and looked around the

pathetic room. "But why am I here? Where am I? This isn't my room."

He lurched upright, his shoulders shifting toward the edge of the bed, his hips staying put, and wailed as Bear crossed the space between them in two strides, to catch him before he fell from the bed.

Bear settled Neatham back against the pillows, and the invalid looked up at him, bewildered. "My legs. What is wrong with my legs?"

No wonder Miss Neatham was worried. *You should never have left the poor, deluded man alone, Miss Neatham. If my roses were so important to you, surely you could have instructed a neighbour to sit with him?* Though there had been no lights in the other cottages.

He searched for something soothing to say. "An injury, I am told, sir. Just rest. Do not let your legs concern you."

Neatham frowned, but did not again attempt to move.

Perhaps Pelman's sister would come in for the night, or—if not—Pelman might know someone. Someone who could change the bedding and dress the man in clean clothes.

Clearly, Neatham couldn't be left alone. Especially not in a house that leaked. A spattering of drops entered around the window each time a gust of wind hit it. A continuous runnel of water down the wall in the corner fell to a pool that grew no bigger, so must be draining away between the floorboards to the room beneath.

"I will fetch help," he told Mr Neatham.

"Fetch the constable," Mr Neatham instructed. "There has been an intruder. I sent Rosie some time ago, but something must have happened to delay her. What did you say your name was?"

"Gavenor," Bear repeated.

"Get the constable, Gavenor," Mr Neatham said. "The man seems to have gone now, but he may come back, and I don't want my wife frightened."

"I will be back as soon as I can, Mr Neatham," Bear said, with little hope that the man would remember.

First, he opened the door at the top of the stairs. A smaller bedroom, clearly Miss Neatham's, even more spartan than the father's. He took down the two gowns hanging on the wall, and manage to fit them into the trunk, which he carried downstairs and left by the door before checking the rooms on that floor. A kitchen with no fire, the few pans old and battered, looking as if they had been salvaged from someone's junk heap. A front room with a single chair at a table by the leaking window, and a woman's work basket, full of folded fabric and sewing paraphernalia. He put that by the trunk. Miss Neatham was clearly used to being occupied.

His coat was still drenched, but he put it on against the worst of the rain. He'd need an oilskin to protect Miss Neatham's possessions while he carried them home. Perhaps Pelman would be able to loan him one.

Climbing back up the hill, dodging the worst of the torrents, he teased at the picture he'd formed, but it didn't make sense. Why on earth was a lady of Miss Neatham's quality living in such a hovel?

Pelman would know, but would he tell Bear? Bear had an uneasy feeling that Pelman knew her story all too well.

CHAPTER 4

A few minutes' walk along the better maintained road at the top of Miss Neatham's alley brought him to Pelman's gate. He soon knocked on the door, which was opened by a maid. She took his coat and hat to hang over a drip tray, and carried off his card to present to her master.

This was more the sort of house where Miss Neatham belonged; a substantial dwelling with several reception rooms and probably a dozen or more bedrooms. The hall in which he waited was wider than the Neatham's entire house, with a handsome staircase at one side broad enough for two people to ascend abreast. Opposite the staircase, portraits and landscapes adorned the wall, with room for half a dozen chairs and several side tables.

Pelman followed the maid back into the hall before Bear had time to do more than glance around.

"Gavenor. What on earth are you doing out in weather like this?"

On the spur of the moment, Bear decided to go fishing. "I'm on a mission for a lady, Pelman. Miss Neatham called on me this afternoon."

Bear didn't miss the worried crease between Pelman's brows, hastily smoothed and replaced with a sneer. "Hah! I might have known she would complain to you. Don't believe her, Gavenor. She has no right to that cottage. None at all."

Pelman gestured. "Come on through to the parlour. You'll want to dry beside the fire. The bi— female must have been convincing to drive you out in this weather." Almost a question, the way his voice rose at the end of the sentence. One Bear had no intention of answering when Pelman spilled so much information without further effort on Bear's part.

Sure enough, the silence prompted him to continue. "Mind you, I don't deny that the baron may have promised the cottage to her— quite likely, under the circumstances—but he put nothing in writing."

Interesting. The ill feeling obviously went both ways. What circumstances made it likely that the baron lied about giving Miss Neatham the cottage? Some men did not consider it dishonourable to lie to their paramours about future benefits, and a wise mistress took her promises in the form of a contract. Gavenor had trouble associating such sordid affairs with his indignant fairy. *Let it sit. Undoubtedly, all will become clear.*

"His will left everything to his nephew, including the cottage and —as I told the lovely Rosabel myself—all its contents. You purchased everything. So, there you are."

Bear resisted the urge to push Miss Neatham's personal name down Pelman's throat, but remained silent, watching Pelman out of the corner of one eye while seemingly intent upon the fire.

"I told her she could take only what she could prove she owned. I was looking out for your interests, Gavenor."

Very revealing. Bear tucked the information away to consider later.

"I am not here about Miss Neatham's housing," he said, as peaceably as he could manage, "though she must find her new accommodations very poor after Rose Cottage. Could you not find her anything more suitable?"

Pelman's tense shoulders relaxed fractionally. "In an instant, if she can afford to pay." His smirk invited Bear to make common cause with him. "You are a businessman, Gavenor. You know how it is. She has no income, and will not be able to afford the place she is in for long. She will need to come to an arrangement with me then."

Bear, guessing what type of arrangement, stood speechless for a moment, fighting to keep from wrapping his hands around Pelman's throat. Over his dead body would his fairy be forced into accepting whatever degrading offer this scum had made.

"Pride is cold comfort when the roof leaks." The new voice was redolent with satisfaction. This would be Pelman's sister. No fairy this one—rather, a hearty country woman with the resemblance to a well-bred horse that seemed characteristic of the type.

Pelman returned his sister's smirk, oblivious to the danger in which he stood. "Livia, allow me to present Mr Gavenor, the gentleman who purchased the Hurley estate. Gavenor, my sister."

Bear bowed. "Charmed, Miss Pelman." A lie, but a social lie.

She simpered. "Mr Gavenor, how delighted we are you have joined our little community." She prattled on about the paucity of social equals and the joys of a visit to Liverpool, not far distant across the Mersey.

The proximity to Liverpool was a prime attraction of the estate. Many of those making their fortunes in Liverpool's shipping and woollen industries wanted a country estate. Their purchase of a second house where they could retreat from the city would mark their arrival in the netherworld between their middle-class origins and the upper classes who would never accept them. Thorne Hall was ideally suited, particularly if the planned steam ferry service was more successful than the one that failed a couple of years earlier.

Bear had spoken to the people behind that project, which was why he had told his agents to look for properties in the Wirral Peninsula. The current Baron Hurley, a London man to the bone, had been glad to get rid of the place he had inherited from his uncle six years ago and visited once since. Bear had paid a price that would make the venture profitable even if he had to raze the ruin to the ground and start again.

Miss Pelman was attempting to discover his plans. He ignored her hints. Time enough to address her disapproval after his plans were accomplished.

"You may be able to help me, Miss Pelman," he said.

She simpered again. "Pelman told me you have need of a house-keeper, Mr Gavenor, and I would be willing to fill the position. On a temporary basis, as a favour. You understand I would need maids to do the actual work, of course." She ran her hands over her gown as if to draw attention to its quality.

Bear shook his head. "I do not need a housekeeper, Miss Pelman. Though it is kind of you to offer."

She frowned. "Oh? Then you have someone?"

"I have my manservant. No, Miss Pelman, that was not the favour. I…" He stopped to consider his words. "I happened to chance upon a Miss Neatham, who has twisted her ankle and is unable to return to her home tonight. I offered to check on her elderly father and found him in some distress. Can you recommend a neighbour who might look after him for the night, until Miss Neatham is able to make appropriate arrangements?" There. That was all true enough without giving this witch some scandal to hold on to.

Miss Pelman's voice became shrill, "Miss Neatham? Rosabel Neatham? Where is she staying? Who is she staying with?"

"A cottager has taken her in," Bear prevaricated. "Terrible weather to be out in, too. The lady is fortunate she was close to somewhere dry."

Miss Pelman snorted like a horse; one that had found something in its feedbag not to its liking. "Lady! Well some might call her a lady, I suppose."

Bear would not allow himself to be distracted. "Mr Neatham, Miss Pelman?"

"I suppose Mrs Able might oblige," Miss Pelman allowed, reluctantly. "She does sick-bed nursing and laying out and the like. I shall give you a note." Suddenly, her frown smoothed and she smiled. "No. Better. Wait for me to get my cape and I shall take you."

Uh oh. Harpy alert. "Thank you. I won't ask you to come out in this rain. A note and directions, and I shall manage."

"Not at all, my dear Mr Gavenor. Why, we are neighbours now, and one must help one's neighbours. I insist. I will be right back."

She fixed him in place with a bright smile. He imagined a crocodile might smile so, all teeth and welcoming joy as its supper approached. Beckoning to her brother, she left the room and Pelman followed, closing the door firmly behind him.

Bear crossed to the door and eased it open. They had not gone farther than the hall, and their voices carried clearly.

"Old Able, Livia?" Pelman sounded both amused and unbelieving.

"It doesn't matter. It is just for a night. But Lawrence, Rose Neatham! If she has got her claws into the first eligible bachelor to arrive in this village in years, I shall scream. Now, where did the rain hood go?"

"Gavenor's not a man for your tricks, Livia," Pelman warned. "Or Rosabel's, either. They call him Bear for his sour disposition. Doesn't have any use for the ladies, by all accounts, except to bed them."

"Nonsense, Lawrence." Miss Pelman sounded farther away this time. Still hunting for the rain hood, perhaps. "He was looking over the Marriage Mart this past Season. My friend Lady Partridge wrote about him. A war hero, she said, and wealthy, and ready to settle down."

Bear remembered Lady Partridge. A sour prune of a woman, disapproving of everything. He pressed his ear to the gap he had created, straining to hear what else she said.

"But whatever he was looking for, he did not find it."

That was true. Bear would like to have his own family. A wife who was a helpmate, and children to cherish. He'd not had that growing up, but it was possible. He needed to look no further than the Earl of Ruthford, once his colonel and now one of his investors.

Ruthford, his wife, and their daughter often welcomed him into their charmed circle when he was in London.

Bear's great aunt had insisted he marry, and in her memory he had gone to look the marriage mart over, but the debutantes made him feel old, and the fashionable widows were either avoiding a second marriage or rapaciously keen hunters who repelled him. He'd become adept at evading traps, but had achieved little else, and had shelved the marriage project for another time.

"He is picky, then," Pelman warned. "Don't pin any hopes on him, Livia."

"He needs a sensible wife, Lady Partridge said," Miss Pelman responded. "One who is accustomed to living in the country but who will show to advantage in social situations, for he is a business-man, Lawrence, and must entertain his clients."

Lady Partridge was more perceptive than Bear had thought, then. That summed his requirements nicely.

Miss Pelman's voice became louder and clearer as she approached the door. "A woman past the silliness of first youth, and a lady born, but not too proud, for the Gavenors are a very obscure family. Gentry, of course, or I would not consider it."

Pelman trailed close behind his sister. "You will do as you wish. You always do."

"I wish I knew where that Neatham pest is staying. Somewhere close to Gavenor, I'll be bound. Twisted ankle. I am surprised such an experienced man was taken in."

Bear hurried away from the door as Miss Pelman's voice drew closer, and was examining a poor imitation of a Ming vase that burdened the mantlepiece when the pair entered the room.

Miss Neatham wore an oiled coat and a matching hood. The hood tied under her chin and had a collar that flared out into a cape to protect her neck and shoulders. "Let us be off, then, Mr Gavenor. You will not wish to be making the trip back to Rose Cottage after dark." She held up a hand and he approached her. "Although… Lawrence, we should offer Mr Gavenor a bed for the night." Again, that crocodile smile. "Lawrence could loan you some things, Mr Gavenor, which would save you a wet and unpleasant trip."

Never. Even if he had not taken on responsibility for Miss Neatham. Now that he'd met the woman and heard her plotting, he had no intention of staying under the same roof as her. He struggled to find courteous words to refuse the offer. "Thank you, Miss Pelman. That is very kind, but I will not consider it. I have left my dinner cooking and would fear to return to a smouldering heap."

Miss Pelman was tenacious. "Lawrence could ride…"

"In this weather?" Pelman objected, glaring at his sister, then sliding his eyes sideways to Bear and rearranging his face into a smile as false as hers. "That is, if you would like to stay, Gavenor, I could send a servant."

"Thank you, but no." Be damned to them if they thought he owed them another reason. "Shall we set out to Mrs Able's, Miss Pelman? That is, unless you would prefer to give me a note and some directions to her house." *Please give me a note and let me escape.*

She led the way from the room. "Yes, yes, let us go. It is not far."

Once out of the gate, Miss Pelman turned uphill, towards the village centre, and then almost immediately down a little narrow side street with four terraced houses on either side. They looked to be of the same vintage and type as the hovels at the bottom of the hill, but in much better condition, and lights flickered behind the downstairs window of each.

Miss Pelman stopped at the second house on the right and mounted the three steps that took the doorway higher than the muddy road. How many people lived here? The cacophony behind the door suggested at least a score: a baby crying, children shouting, and a couple of adult voices pitched to be heard above all the rest.

A knock brought an immediate response: a child's voice retreating as it shouted, "Mam, Mam, someone's to door."

The door opened, just enough for a half-grown girl to insert her wiry body in the gap and examine first Miss Pelman and then Bear with eyes that were twenty years older than the rest of her.

"We're here to see your mother," Miss Pelman did not waste courtesy on the children of the poor. "Take us to her."

The girl let the door swing open and led the way a few paces down the narrow, cluttered hall to a parlour door. Five children of various ages and sizes tumbled up and down the stairs leading to the upper floor, playing some complicated game that required frequent pauses for negotiation of the next move. In the parlour, more children draped themselves across the furniture, sat against the walls, or lay on their stomachs on the knotted rag rugs.

A lushly built woman, not old enough to be mother of all these children, let the suckling infant she held detach itself from her nipple, and reached for the wailing baby that one of the older girls held. Another girl scooped up the little sprite who had finished his or her meal, and skirted Bear to whisk it out of the room.

The nursing woman watched Bear with a sardonic eye, as if daring him to comment on her exposed, full breasts. He kept his face impassive as the baby in her arms bumped blindly against her bare skin. She thrust her nipple into its wailing mouth, silencing, at least, that source of noise.

"Mam Able, it's Miss Pelman and a gentleman," the door opener announced, and Bear turned to see who was being addressed.

Half screened by children, another woman watched them from one of the couches. She was much older. The first woman's mother, perhaps? They shared the same eyes, though this second woman had run to fat, with several chins, a bosom like the prow of a ship and arms like young oaks. Above her broad face, hair an unlikely shade of orange stuck out in a parody of a fashionable coiffure.

"Wha' might Miss Pelman 'n' a gen'leman want of Mrs Able?" she asked, tipping her head to one side in question.

Miss Pelman drew herself up to announce, "Mrs Able, Mr Gavenor is a great friend of my brother's, and he has need of your services." She ignored the nursing mother as if she were not in the room.

Bear regretted his keen sense of smell, which detected urine-wet child, heavy sweat, and an overlay of juniper. Gin, probably.

"Lying in, laying out, wet nurse, or sick-bed nurse? Only, if you need a wet nurse, you'll 'ave to 'ave Penny." She gestured to the woman feeding the baby, explaining, "Me dugs 'ave dried." Miss

Pelman glanced in the direction of the gesture and as quickly looked away.

"Sick-bed nurse," Bear told her. "Just for the night, until the daughter can make other arrangements."

"It is Neatham," Miss Pelman explained. "But Mr Gavenor is paying."

Mrs Able pursed her lips. "Just tonight?"

Bear nodded.

"Two shillings by the night. Extra if he soils himself."

Highway robbery, but undoubtedly anyone with this many mouths to feed needed the money. "Half now, half in the morning."

"And dinner from the inn and a pint of porter."

He would pass the inn on his way back to Rose Cottage. "I will pay to have it sent. Enough for Mr Neatham, too."

The sick-bed nurse hoisted herself from her seat. "Penny, they're all yours," she announced.

Penny cast her eyes upwards, though whether in prayer or protest, Bear couldn't say. "I've someone I promised to meet tomorrow, noonish," she warned.

"I'll be back by then, or Sal can watch them."

Mrs Able left the room to a chorus of "Night, Mam," and pulled on some men's boots in the hall while the children on the stairs stopped long enough to add their good nights.

Then she covered her head and shoulders with a blanket before leading the way back across to the Pelhams' street and to the entrance of a steep flight of steps that led down to the hollow where the Neathams' new abode wallowed in its pond.

Miss Pelman looked uncertainly down the hill to the waiting flood. Bear seized his chance. "Thank you for your help, Miss Pelman. I'll just stand here, shall I? Until you are safely within your doors."

She looked at him helplessly, but the wind blew a sudden flurry of heavy drops into the face sheltered under her rain hood. "Yes, of course. Do please call again, Mr Gavenor. I will tell Pelman that he must invite you for dinner."

She hurried off down the street, and he watched dutifully until her front door closed behind her, wondering how influential the Pelmans were in the local community. Could he avoid a closer association and still do business here?

"Are you coming, Mr Gavenor?" the sick-bed nurse called from halfway down the steps. He collected himself and followed, and soon re-entered the miserable house.

CHAPTER 5

Mr Gavenor was gone for a very long time; so long, that Rosa began to wonder if he intended to return. Rosa managed to scoot across the floor on her bottom to fetch a book to pass the time. Getting back up on the couch seemed too much trouble, so she remained on the rug, leaning against what used to be her chair.

The book was an old favourite, but it couldn't engage her interest, which kept hopping back to the pain in her ankle and her anxiety about her father. A little about Mr Gavenor, too. She hoped he had not come to harm. Not that she wished to stay the night in his cottage, but he seemed a kind man, if a little gruff.

All right. A lot gruff. Oddly enough, that reassured her. The kind of facile charm that Pelman turned on as if with a tap hid a familiar danger, for he expected to be rewarded with liberties she had no intention of permitting. Not, at least, from Pelman, for though she was running out of other ways to protect and care for her father, he was not the only man in England. If she must sell herself to someone, it would not be to the man who had driven her to such a necessity.

Except she had not the first idea how to find another man who might want a virgin well past her youth—and one with few feminine graces.

Once again, Rosa reviewed the litany of her marketable skills.

She could teach reading and writing, but the Pelmans had convinced the locals she was not fit to associate with children.

She could make botanical observations and illustrate them with drawings. She had thought she might be able to sell a pamphlet, or perhaps even a book, but her hopes were dashed when the printer to whom she sent samples returned an enthusiastic letter that raised her hopes then dashed them with a quote for the money she must advance. Apparently, authors must pay the costs for publication and distribution. The sum required was more than she had seen in one place in her entire lifetime.

She could sew neatly, although without enthusiasm. Sewing currently kept them alive, since those who could afford a seamstress preferred to hire someone for the long seams of their gowns, at the very least. The employment paid a pittance, but even a pittance was better than nothing.

For the rest, she could translate from and to Greek and Roman, and make a reasonable fist of Hebrew. Baron Hurley had often given her such work to do; yes, and paid her, too, for all that she was woman, but Lord Hurley had been dead for years, and no one else wanted an informally trained female translator.

She could keep house, if anyone wanted a housekeeper tainted with scandal and burdened by a bedridden father who constantly mistook her for her mother or her aunt. After Thorne Hall was damaged by fire, she kept house at Rose Cottage for her father. She'd been feeding them mostly from her garden, her goats, and her hens, all of which Pelman had confiscated when he had thrown her and her father out.

She had considered complaining to the squire about Pelman trampling on her rights, but the residents of Thorne Hall and Sir Gerard's family had been estranged for as long as she could remember, though she had never heard why. The squire was known as a fair man, if hard. He would uphold the law. If Rosa had something to prove the law was on her side, she would swallow her pride and pay him a visit.

But without evidence, she would not get a fair hearing from a man who seemed to hate her just because she was the previous Lord Hurley's librarian's daughter.

Unfortunately, as that horrid sneak Pelman had said, she had only her word that she owned the goats, both presents from Lord Hurley. He had gone on to point out that the garden was part of the cottage, and if she took the hens, where would she put them? Then, mightily condescending, he had given her ten shillings in compensation for four fine layers and a bantam that was sitting on eggs.

Rosa had taken the money. She needed it to keep them fed. A fortnight, her hens had bought her. Perhaps three weeks. Six of those days were now gone.

How did the hens fare in this dreadful weather? Perhaps she would be able to see them from the scullery window.

She employed the bottom-shuffling method to make her way to the hall and the umbrella stand, then pulled herself up so that she could collect the walking stick. Leaning heavily on that, hobbling to keep as much weight off her foot as possible, Rosa made her way to the kitchen, where a pot simmered on the fire, and then through to the scullery. Sheets of rain obscured her view into the back garden, each wind gust battering water against the window panes.

Between the rain and the hens' reluctance to be out in such weather, she'd see nothing this afternoon. Now that she was up, however, she could steep some willow-bark tea. Mr Gavenor had returned her basket to the larder, aligning it as precisely to the edge as she would have herself.

She scanned the shelves, noting gaps where her stores of food had been depleted. Pelman, no doubt, helping himself to anything that appealed. She could find no milk and none of the goat's cheese she had been forced to leave behind. The basket she kept for fresh eggs held half a dozen. The lay from the last two days? If so, the hens were well, and she certainly didn't grudge the eggs to Mr Gavenor, if he was the one who collected them. Not after his kindness to her.

Mr Gavenor's hands had been so gentle when he examined, and later wrapped, her ankle. For all his size, his touch was delicate, and it had been generous of him to go out into the storm to assuage her worries.

What could be keeping him so long? The stew was evidence he intended to return. With one hand, she set a kettle of water to boil while balancing her weight on the walking stick, then stirred the stew. It smelt wonderful, but would taste even better with a couple of potatoes baked in the ashes. This year's crop, she thought, would be rotting in the inhospitable ground, but she limped into the larder and reached to the bottom of the storage box to fetch two potatoes from the previous year's harvest.

While she was at it, she cored two apples and filled the holes with a spoonful of honey and some black currant jam. She placed the filled apples in a small pot nestled among the embers. They would make a nice, sweet dish with dinner.

There. She should sit again. Her ankle throbbed so she could barely think, but, at least, Mr Gavenor would come home to a hot meal.

CHAPTER 6

Bear's mood lifted as he topped the last rise in the road and saw Rose Cottage. It's tiled roof glowed in the sun, which had dropped below the clouds as it set in the west. He'd been much longer than he'd expected, but, at least, the rain had stopped.

Mr Neatham's reaction to the nurse had been gruelling. He'd objected to being washed and changed, fighting weakly and finishing in helpless tears. "Who are you?" he kept asking. "Why are you doing this?"

Mrs Able had been firm but kind, which made Bear feel a little better. He'd sent a good meal from the inn, enough food for both nurse and patient. He'd been tempted to stop and have some himself, but he'd put a stew on that morning, to simmer by the fire, and needed to get back. Miss Neatham was on her own, and injured.

He let himself in the front door and looked into his study. No Miss Neatham. The blanket he'd draped over her was there, but the woman was gone. For a moment, he heard Miss Pelman's voice again, "I am surprised such an experienced man was taken in."

No. She could not have faked the swelling and bruising. Still, if she had made her way up to his bed like that foolish woman at the

Ruthford' house party, she would be very disappointed in his response.

He crossed to the formal parlour, opposite his study. No Miss Neatham. At the back of the house, the little room that had been set up as a workroom, and on the other side of the stairs, the kitchen. There, he found Miss Neatham, asleep in a chair at the kitchen table, her injured foot resting on one of the benches.

Bear stood looking down at her. He was not good at judging the ages of females, but he thought she must be of similar years to Miss Pelman. Perhaps a few years younger, or perhaps it was just that her face was pleasanter, without the sour lines that Miss Pelman's disposition had carved into her visage as outward warnings to the unwary.

He glanced down at the ankle, which had swollen more despite the bandage. Obviously, she had been walking on it. What had she been up to? He picked up the cup at her elbow and sniffed at the bitter tea. Willow bark. He should have thought of that himself.

Next, he checked the kitchen fire, and soon found the two potatoes baking in the embers and the pot with its apples, stewed into a fragrant mush. A busy lady, his invalid.

Rosa jerked awake at the sound of china clinking in the scullery. By the time Mr Gavenor appeared in the doorway, she had remembered where she was, and why, and was sitting up, rearranging her gown to hide her ankle.

"You are awake," Mr Gavenor said. "Good. I'm starving." He put two plates on the table and turned back to the fire. Swiftly and efficiently, a pot mitt on his hand, he swung the stew off the fire and lifted it to the pot stand that sat ready on the table.

Rosa leaned forward. "My father? How is my father?"

He glanced at her, and then focused on the potatoes he fished from the embers with a long pair of tongs. "You didn't tell me he was senile."

"He's not sen…" *But he is, and increasingly so.* "He gets confused, and he forgets things, but some days he is quite…"

Mr Gavenor ignored her demurrals. "I hired someone to stay with him for the night."

Rosa winced at the thought of her diminishing store of hen money. "I cannot afford…"

Mr Gavenor ladled stew over the potatoes he had cut, unruffled by her protests. "My responsibility. If I had not startled you, you would not have fallen, and you would be home with him now. Here. Eat."

He pushed a plate over in front of her and slid the other to the place he'd set for himself, then pulled out the chair so he could sit down.

Rosa folded her hands in her lap, bowed her head, and murmured a request for blessing on the food and the cook, then looked up to find Mr Gavenor observing her, his fork in his hand, his eyes alive with interest in an expressionless face.

"Thank you," she told him. "It is very kind of you."

He looked down at his plate and dug his fork into the stew. "Potatoes were a good idea, but you should have kept to the couch. That ankle won't heal if you keep putting weight on it."

Gruff. But I have your measure, Mr Gavenor. You are a kind man. "I meant, thank you for hiring someone. Whom did you find?"

Mr Gavenor shrugged. "Miss Pelman recommended a Mrs Able. A rough woman, but she seems kind enough."

Miss Pelman. What did she say about me? Nothing pleasant, that is certain. "Mrs Able is kind. But she drinks. A lot."

"I noticed." Mr Gavenor further proved her opinion of him by expanding on that wry observation. "I stayed until your father was comfortable. Toward the end, he seemed to know her. I will check again in the morning."

Mr Gavenor finished his plateful of stew and potatoes in silence, then frowned at the amount left on her plate. "I am full, sir," she explained. A little nauseous from the headache, and considerably smaller than the giant, who had not taken their size difference into account in his serving portions.

"You are a dainty little thing," he observed. He ladled more stew onto his own plate and said, with every evidence of satisfaction, "And apples for after."

It had been tasty and filling, but hardly an elegant meal. Rosa had managed much better when her larder had been full, which reminded her of her latest grievance against Pelman. "I was going to make a custard, but the milk is all gone."

He cocked a brow. "You had a cow?"

"Goats. Three goats; two nannies, one with a kid at hoof." A female, which she had planned to keep to expand the amount of milk and cheese she could sell.

"No goats here," Mr Gavenor said. "Just the hens." He looked at her thoughtfully. "You had no room for the goats in that horrible hovel?"

It is a horrible hovel, but what choice do I have? Resentment made Rosa's voice sharp, "Mr Pelman insisted the goats belonged to you, Mr Gavenor, so I suggest you apply to him for their return."

"I see." He took her plate and his through to the scullery, came back with two bowls, and busied himself with serving the apples. She waited for further comment, but he said nothing. *He sees? What does he see?* A great deal, she was beginning to think. Behind that still, calm face, a busy mind weighed facts and drew conclusions.

She accepted her apple, and enjoyed the mix of sweet and tart.

"Which was your bedchamber when you were here, Miss Neatham?" Mr Gavenor asked, once he had cleared his bowl. Rosa looked up, startled by the broken silence.

"I will take your trunk up and make up the bed. You sit here and keep your ankle up."

He had brought her trunk?

"The back room on the left, overlooking the vegetable garden," she said. "I do not know what to say. 'Thank you' seems so inadequate."

Mr Gavenor shrugged off her gratitude. "My fault you fell. My responsibility to make sure you and your father are cared for."

He took her bowl into the scullery then returned to give her orders, emphasizing his points with his fingers. "No moving. No putting more stress on that ankle. Do not even think about doing the dishes. I want you well and gone as soon as may be, Miss Neatham. How is your head feeling?"

"The willow bark tea helped," she prevaricated. *Sore, and I will be glad to be in bed.*

"Another cup before bed," he suggested. "I will put the kettle on before I go upstairs."

He suited action to words, then left her alone in the kitchen with her thoughts and a final warning about staying in one place and not moving her ankle.

Gruff, but kind.

CHAPTER 7

The storm returned in the night, and they woke to persistent rain.

Bear carried Miss Neatham downstairs and set her up in the parlour with a book to read and strict instructions not to move. She proceeded to fret herself to flinders, though she tried not to show it. Each time he went in to ask her where to find something, or to bring her something to eat or drink, or just to check that she was following instructions, he could read the anxiety about her father on her open face.

He'd seen her bite back words all morning. "When will you go to the village?" she did not say, but the question was written clearly for Bear to see—a supposition she confirmed with her deep sigh of relief when he said, "The rain looks as if it is clearing. I'll go down to the village now, Miss Neatham. I have a few things to buy, and I will check on your father."

It felt good to stretch his legs. He'd chosen the bed chamber with the largest bed, but even that wasn't big enough for a man of his frame. Still, he'd slept in worse. If it was too narrow and too short, the mattress was comfortable, and the linen clean, if much mended.

Evidence of the night's storm met his eyes all along the road, in deeper puddles and streams, downed tree branches, and flattened crops. He'd be wise to plan for more rain to come, and should buy what they needed while he could.

Miss Neatham had clearly been a provident housekeeper, for the house was fully stocked with all the staples, but they could do with the milk she had mentioned last night and some fresh bread. He'd buy more meat, too. He could not help but draw the conclusion that her financial situation took a dire turn for the worse thanks to Pelman's intervention on his behalf.

He would have to see how the situation could be corrected. Also, he needed to find out if Mrs Able was available for another week or so. Otherwise, Miss Neatham would go home to that horrid little hovel and put her ankle at risk by looking after the old man herself.

Probably best to check on the old man first. In the village's main street, straw had been laid on the worst mud patches, but the steep alley to Miss Neatham's abode was scoured into treacherous ruts, so he kept to the sides where a few inches of relatively dry ground gave his boots better purchase.

The quavering voice of the old man raised in a shriek distracted him from his focus on his footing. "Help! Murder! Help!" Neatham shouted.

Probably nothing, Bear concluded as he hastened his steps, leaping the puddles on his way to the door. When he burst in the door, not bothering to knock, he heard the sound of a slap, and Miss Pelman's voice hissing, "Keep your mouth shut, you filthy old man, or you'll get another one."

Bear slowed so he could ghost up the stairs, setting each foot down gently but with all haste until he stood in the shadows of the hall, peering into the room where Miss Pelman bent threateningly over the bed where Neatham cowered. The stink of bodily wastes filled the room, and Bear's heart turned over with pity.

In the corner, Mrs Able snored, an empty gin bottle lying on its side by her feet. The fire he'd lit the night before was nothing but embers, but the room was warm enough.

"I won't be cleaning you up, and don't you think it," Miss

Pelman told him. "Even that fool Gavenor wouldn't expect it of me. Now eat this breakfast so I can tell him I've looked after you."

"I want my Rosie," Neatham whimpered.

"Your Rosie is dead, and a good thing too," Miss Pelman told him. "She was a whore like her sister, and so is her daughter. Hah! Try to hit me, would you? Take that!"

Before she could return Neatham's ineffectual swing with a blow of her own, Bear moved swiftly into the room and grabbed her raised hand.

"No, Miss Pelman," he said.

She turned, twisting under his restraining hand, perhaps more quickly than she intended because her face was still contorted in rage before she consciously smoothed it into a polite smile. "Why, Mr Gavenor. I did not expect you. Have you walked all the way here again? How conscientious you are. I do admire a responsible man." The simper she tried looked utterly out of place on her face.

"Miss Pelman, I suggest you leave." He managed to hold on to his temper, but only just.

"Leave, Mr Gavenor? But I was giving Mr Neatham his breakfast. I am sorry to say that Mrs Able is indisposed, and I was sure you would wish me to help out." She assayed a smile.

Bear took a deep breath. "I have been listening to you abuse this poor, sick man, and I want you out of here."

"Out," Mr Neatham agreed. "Not you, lad. Pelman's little girl, if that's who she really is. You can stay, whatever-your-name-is. You're the boy who was here yesterday. Lord Hurley's valet. You helped me get dressed."

Miss Pelman opened her mouth to object, but Bear took a step away from her and roared, "Out!" She jumped and scurried toward the door, saying over her shoulder, "You are making a bad mistake, Mr Gavenor."

Left alone with Mr Neatham and the sleeping Mrs Able, Bear regarded Mr Neatham carefully. Now what?

"Lad," Mr Neatham said, his voice dropping into a confidential whisper, "Lad, I have a bit of a problem. Hurley and I—we must have dipped a bit deep last night, and I'm afraid I've… Things are a bit of a mess, and my legs don't seem to want to work."

It would not be the first time he'd served a friend so. "That's all right, Mr Neatham. We'll have you cleaned up and comfortable in no time."

He'd left a bucket of water in the fireplace, and when he checked, it remained half full of warm water. Good enough. Now for some rags to wash the old man, and clean clothes to change him into.

Mr Neatham, happy with his own explanation for Bear's presence, chatted cheerfully while Bear washed him. "You're a big fellow. Haven't been a valet for long, have you? Army, I'm guessing?"

"You would be right, sir. I've been army since I was a boy."

"You're doing very well, mind," Neatham reassured him. "And Hurley's a good man to serve. Pays well, and reasonable in what he asks. What's your name, lad? I didn't quite catch it."

Perhaps the poor soul would retain a simpler name. "Most people call me Bear, sir." Even his own family, back in the dim past, when he'd been a child. In fact, the nickname had been bestowed by his sister, two years his elder and shorter than him, before he was out of skirts. His mother had told him so, many times. "She called you Bear, because you were big and slow and clumsy. You still are, Bear."

Mr Neatham accepted the nickname with a grin that took years off his age. "Bear, is it? Well, I can see why, a big fellow like you."

The rain had set in again before Bear arrived back at Rose Cottage. He'd told the innkeeper's son, Georgie, whom he'd hired with the gig, the same vague story about Miss Neatham staying in the place where she'd been injured, adding that he'd offered to make sure Neatham was cared for, and was taking the man back to Rose Cottage where Bear's servants would see to him.

The fabrication was not quite a cloak of respectability, but it was the best he could do, and spoilt as soon as they drew up at the cottage and Miss Neatham looked out the window of the parlour.

With one eye on Georgie, who was attending to the horses, he made shooing motions, and she withdrew into the shadows.

He carried Neatham into the house, taking him into the study and settling him on a couch.

"You make yourself comfortable, Mr Neatham. I'll just finish bringing in the luggage."

The journey had tired the old man, and his eyelids drooped even as Bear left the room. Good. Now, if Miss Neatham could contain her impatience for a short while longer, they might brush through.

Georgie stood in the entrance hall, gaping around, holding the first of the bags and pillowcases that Bear had stuffed with as many of the Neathams' possessions as he could find. They would not be going back to that hovel, if he had anything to say about it, and he expected the neighbours, starting with Mrs Able, to lift anything not nailed down as soon as he left the shack.

"Just put them in the corner, Georgie. My man will sort them later."

The illusion of a house full of servants was probably a lost cause, now that Georgie had set foot inside. He could only hope the youth was both stupid and suggestible.

They trudged in and out of the rain, until the gig was offloaded, and the pathetic heap of belongings sat dripping in its own puddle in the corner.

"Thank you." Bear handed over the agreed florin, and Georgie took it, bit it, and put it away somewhere about his person. He then put out his hand again.

"Bit more to it, Mr Gavenor, weren't there? Reckon another of those would be fair."

"You have what we agreed, Georgie. I've paid your father for the horse and gig, and a florin to you to drive it."

Bear's scowl didn't bother the boy. "Thing is, Mr Gavenor, I reckon you don't want me telling folks what I saw as I drove up. Who I saw, I should say. I reckon that's worth another florin."

In a moment, the lad was up against the wall, dangling by the throat from Bear's large hand. "I don't pay blackmail, young man. You will keep your tongue between your teeth, or I shall find you and rip it out. Do we understand one another?"

He dropped the lad, who choked an agreement and scurried out the door.

Bear sighed. There was not a snowball's chance in hell that young Georgie would keep the titillating piece of gossip to himself. Bear shrugged. He could do nothing about it.

CHAPTER 8

Rosa listened, her ear pressed to the door. Mr Gavenor would castigate her for not having her foot up, but she wouldn't mind that. He'd brought Papa here!

Papa's arrival would not save her reputation, which had been fragile before someone revived the old rumours about her aunt, and was now in tatters, but his presence eased her mind. She restrained herself, but was in a fever of impatience by the time George from the inn achieved his rapid departure. As soon as she was sure he had really departed, she hobbled into the hall.

"You should have your foot up," Mr Gavenor growled.

"How can I ever thank you? How is my father?"

"Sleeping, Miss Neatham. I put him on the couch in the study. If it will make you feel better, you can settle yourself in there while I tidy up a bit." He glared at the pile of packages in the corner as if their condition represented a personal affront.

She took in the little pile of bags and pillowcases. "Oh dear."

"Yes." Mr Gavenor twisted his mouth and bowed his head. "I am sorry. There was no way to bring them without things getting wet, and I did not trust your neighbours not to break down the door and strip the house bare once I left."

"Of course. You are right." Rosa had not meant to sound critical. "I could not be more grateful, and a little water will not hurt."

He looked up at her from under his brows. "I wrapped the books and put them as safely as I could in your father's trunk. Anything else that might be damaged by water, too."

Right. To work then. "Towels to take up the worst of it, and then we can spread the clothes and linens to dry in the spare bedchamber. Fortunately, we do not have a lot." She reached the heap, lifted the items on top and began to sort them into things that were barely damp, things that could easily be wiped dry, and things that would require wringing out and then hanging.

Mr Gavenor hovered over her, his hands opening and closing as if he could barely keep himself from picking her up and carting her off to the parlour.

"Miss Neatham, I insist that you sit down. If you must help put all of this to rights, I will bring the things to you."

"Perhaps you could bring me a chair, then, Mr Gavenor," she suggested, "so we don't spread puddles through the rest of the house."

For some reason, her request tickled his sense of humour. One corner of his mouth quirked up in a smile, and his eyes gleamed before he strode off to the parlour and returned with two chairs. "One for your foot," he explained, positioning them. "I will fetch some towels."

"The old patched ones from the bottom shelf, please," she commanded, and was rewarded with another amused glance.

A bossy fairy. He had never imagined such a thing, but he rather liked it. He knew where he stood with Miss Neatham; somewhat higher than Pelman and cockroaches, but considerably lower than her father and the missing goats. She was unlike any Society lady he'd ever met.

Apart from Lady Ruthford, who had been a merchant's

daughter and then an army wife, and who retained the kind of practical good sense that a man like Bear appreciated. And his great aunt, of course. She had been another no-nonsense lady who said what she meant and did not try to cajole or manipulate him. Unless the grumpy note left with her will was manipulation.

> *"Do not be a fool and avoid marriage just because the examples you have seen are poor. And do not avoid women because of your mother. She was a stupid woman, and a selfish one. She made my nephew unhappy, and she made you miserable. I have left my house to your daughter, great-nephew, so find a decent woman you can be happy with and grow me an heiress. A legitimate child, if you please. I am not encouraging immorality."*

I tried, Aunt Clara. I tried.

The lawyer who had brought him Aunt Clara's will had explained he could challenge the provision, since he had neither wife nor child, but Aunt Clara had been the only person in his family to care whether he lived or died, and surely it was not too much for her to ask him to marry? He would have to try again, and he dreaded the idea.

Together, he and Miss Neatham sorted their way through the Neatham's possessions, him handing her things to fold or to dry, taking others out into the covered porch so he could wring as much water as possible from them.

"I owe you an apology, Miss Neatham," Bear said, after a while. "I asked Pelman to find me somewhere to stay close to Thorne Hall, which led to you being turned from your home."

She looked up from the trinket box she wiped, startled. "You did not know I existed, I imagine."

"I did not. But I know now, and feel some responsibility."

She tipped her head slightly, her brow creasing. "You have been very kind, Mr Gavenor, but you are not responsible for me. It seems we must share this roof, at least until I can make other arrangements. Let us just leave it at that. That pile of linen in the buckets?

There is a drying rack in the lean-to off the stable. Would you fetch it when next the rain stops, and set it up in the spare bed chamber?"

Bear had expected financial demands, or the command to leave her house immediately, or even (if Pelman's hints held any truth) a proposition that he take the part of protector, a role into which Pelman had been trying to bully his way. No. That was just a fantasy of his base self. He would lay odds that she was nearly as innocent as she appeared.

CHAPTER 9

Over the next three days, they fell into a routine. Mr Gavenor refused to allow Rosa to look after her father at night, but carried them both downstairs to the parlour each morning. Rosa sat close enough to attend to the invalid when he needed a drink or to have his chin wiped, to talk or read to him, to continue with the sewing in the work basket Mr Gavenor had carried home on his first trip, and to carry out the little tasks she begged Mr Gavenor for while her father slept.

"I am perfectly capable of peeling vegetables, mixing batter, and sewing that button back on your waistcoat," she insisted, and he quirked his smile at her and gave in.

Whenever the rain stopped for more than a few minutes, he left them to walk over to Thorne Hall. "I am no builder," he told Rosa, "but I've learned a few things in the last year or two. I need to get some idea of the number of local men I'll need to hire when my work crew arrives from Liverpool, and that depends on what can be saved, and what must be demolished."

He made copious notes in a small notebook, which he transcribed into a large ledger each evening.

Father was comfortable with him, which was a blessing, since Mr

Gavenor took over all of the embarrassing personal services, at least when he was home.

"He's a good lad, this man Lord Hurley sent," Father said. He had never lost the habit of speaking in front of the servants as if they were deaf, and he was convinced Mr Gavenor was a servant, though some days he thought him a valet or footman from Thorne Hall, and others he went further back in his memories to his days at Cambridge and even to his childhood.

At least twenty times a day, he asked Mr Gavenor his name, and each time received the patient reply, "They call me 'Bear,' sir."

Father usually called her Rosie, though sometimes even that dearly loved name escaped him.

"Rosie is short for Rosemary, which was my mother's name," she explained to Mr Gavenor after dinner one evening, while Father dozed in his chair. "I am told I look a little like her. And, of course, I am much the same age as she was when she died."

Rosa and Mr Gavenor relaxed in separate chairs on either side of the hearthrug. Rosa held a glass of blackberry cordial, and Mr Gavenor, a glass of brandy.

"You must have been just a little girl," Mr Gavenor said.

"Eleven. It has been nearly twenty-five years and I still miss her. So does Father, of course. She was the great love of his life."

Mr Gavenor took a sip of brandy, his long fingers caressing the glass. "Did you come to live at Thorne Hall after she died?"

"Oh no. My father was librarian there when he married Mama, and Lord Hurley gave them private apartments in the library wing. I grew up at Thorne Hall." An only child, she had a playmate and companion in her mother. Lord Hurley and her father kept busy about their own affairs.

Her mother and both men insisted that she was a lady, and she was not allowed to play with the children on the local farms. Nor was she welcome at the only other home within easy reach that had a child of a similar age. No one had ever explained the source of the feud between Threxton Grange and Thorne Hall, but Rosa knew the futility of asking to play with the boy and two girls growing up in that family. Instead, she peopled her world from her imagination. Her friends were the portraits and animal heads on the walls of Thorne Hall, and the people in the books in the library that was her father's charge and passion.

Then Mama died. For months beforehand, she had been teaching Rosa the tasks that made up her daily life, and her last words to her daughter were, "Look after your father."

"I was eleven," she repeated. "Old enough to take charge of our apartments. Old enough to make sure that Father remembered to eat and had everything he needed to do credit to his position."

Mr Gavenor seemed about to speak, but changed his mind and took another sip of brandy.

Rosa hastened to add, "He has always been so absorbed in his work, you see." She took a small mouthful of blackberry cordial and let the rich flavours seep across her tongue. The role of audience had always been hers. An interested listener was a new experience and seduced her into explaining, "Lord Hurley and Father built the library between them, but Father was the one who loved the books for what they contained. Lord Hurley was a collector. He wanted the oldest, the rarest, the most unusual. He wanted to boast to other book lovers about the treasures he had found. Father wanted to understand the people and times the books described, and the people who wrote them. Lord Hurley used to say they made a good team, for Lord Hurley had the money to indulge Father's passion and Father had the knowledge to make Lord Hurley's reputation."

"It sounds like a lonely life for a young girl," Mr Gavenor observed.

Was she lonely? She missed her mother, of course, but she had always been alone except for the servants, her parents, and Lord Hurley. "I had the servants for company, and I spent a lot of time in the library. Father taught me Greek and Roman so that I could transcribe his notes for him. Hebrew, too, before his mind began to fail. We even used to take our meals in there. Father found it hard to leave the library when he was on the trail of something new. Lord Hurley would join us sometimes, and he always had amusing stories to tell."

"You said you moved to Rose Cottage eight years ago. Was that when your father could no longer care for the library?"

Rosa shuddered. "He almost set it on fire," she said. "He had always been forgetful. I really did not realize how bad he had become until the night he set every candle he could find burning in the library. If Lord Hurley had not wanted to check a reference, one of them might well have caught a drapery or paper… He and Father woke me, arguing. Father insisted Lord Hurley was trying to burn the books, which was nonsense, of course."

Once again, Mr Gavenor said nothing.

"We tried to keep him in his apartment. Lord Hurley appointed a footman to follow him everywhere. He grew more confused about where he was and when. In his own mind, he and Mama were young again. He began to wander at night, looking for Mama, or perhaps for something else. In the end, Lord Hurley gave us the cottage so I could keep him safe."

'G ave,' she said, but not in writing, according to Pelman. Bear knew that the new Baron Hurley had succeeded his great uncle six years ago. He'd told Bear that he'd been to see the estate once. "It was a disappointment, I don't mind telling you, Gavenor. I knew my uncle was a warm man, but most of his fortune was tied up in books. The money pretty much went up in smoke the night my uncle died. The whole library wing was gutted."

The fire had not killed Hurley, who had been found in his room on the undamaged side of the house. "The shock of the fire," his successor thought, though Bear wondered how the old lord had known about the fire if he was on the other side of the house, and why he stayed in his bed chamber if he did know.

Had Neatham anything to do with that fire? As if prompted by his thought, Miss Neatham said, "Of course, when Lord Hurley died, we lost the servants he sent to look after us, but I have managed well enough. Except, once Father no longer had a footman sleeping in the same room, he used to wander when he woke in the night. That is how he hurt his back. He'd go to Thorne Hall, looking for the library or Lord Hurley or Mama, and two years ago, he was upstairs in our old apartments when the floor collapsed."

Her eyes filled with an old grief and she lowered them, put her glass down and picked up the piece of sewing lying atop her workbasket.

Bear still wondered about the fire, but she clearly needed a change of topic. "A new gown?" he asked, nodding toward her busy hands.

"Yes, for Mrs Raby at Three Oaks. Her Sunday-best gown. I promised it to her for next weekend, and I still have four more long seams to go." She glared at the fabric as her busy needle darted in and out.

So, Miss Neatham, born to the gentry, scholar of Greek and Latin, raised in the biggest manor house in the neighbourhood, took in sewing for farmers' wives. Bear managed to keep a frown from his face, but not by much. Lord Hurley and Neatham had not done well by Miss Neatham.

CHAPTER 10

The next day had long, fine spells between rain showers, and Bear was able to spend most of the day at Thorne Hall. He came home with a pocketful of notes to the appetizing aroma of roast meat.

He frowned at Miss Neatham from the doorway of the parlour. She sat in the chair where he had left her, her foot propped up, the picture of demure obedience. "You have been in the kitchen, Miss Neatham," he growled.

She smiled, not one whit discomforted by his tone or his scold. "You have been out in the rain, Mr Gavenor, and will be glad of a warm meal."

Bear surrendered to the grin that kept trying to break out. "Not a great deal of rain, today. When it started again, I walked home." No. Not home. A brief stopover while he got on with his job, for all that he had spent the day resisting the urge to return to the warmth of Miss Neatham's nurturing care.

He looped back the curtain to show her the rain pattering against the glass, then stilled. "Miss Neatham, stay out of sight. There's a visitor coming to the door."

The rider—anonymous in a heavy rain cape and hood—

dismounted, tied his horse to the gate post, and opened the gate. Bear went into the hall and shut the parlour door behind him, ready to open the front door when the knock came.

The caller was Pelman. *Of course, it was.* "Gavenor. I rode up to see how you are. My sister was concerned about you, all the way out here on your own." The man did his best to peer over and around Bear, who blocked as much of the doorway as he could.

"Kind of her, Pelman. But—as you see—I am well."

"Can I come in for a minute and dry off?" Pelman asked. "I am as wet as a fish."

Bear could think of no reasonable way to refuse, little though he wanted to invite the man in. "Yes. Yes, of course. Come through to the study and I will pour you a brandy."

"Thank you. I don't like the look of the bridge back down the road a bit. If that goes, you'll be cut off. Best come stay with us, Gavenor." Pelman followed him down the hall. Thank the gods, Miss Neatham was a tidy soul and insisted on everything being put away where it belonged. He opened the study door and ushered Pelman inside. "Yes, pack a bag, my dear fellow," Pelman said, "and come back with me. We have plenty of room."

"I will not, though I thank you for the invitation." Bear had many reasons for declining the invitation, and—unless he missed his guess—any he shared with Pelman would soon be spread through the whole village. "I have all I need here, and the rain cannot last forever. I can get out during the clear spells and I've made a start on surveying what the manor needs in the way of repairs. If I move into the village, I'll be too far away to fit my work around the weather."

"Well, if you say so." Pelman accepted the offered brandy and took an immediate swig, not waiting for it to warm. "To be honest, I thought I might find you tucked up in a love nest with Rosa Neatham. No one in the village has seen her since before the storm started, and you carried her father off a few days ago, apparently."

Disgusting maggot. Apparently, he had misjudged young Georgie, or the whole village would know precisely where Miss

Neatham and her father were living. "Which I would hardly have done if Miss Neatham was my mistress, Pelman."

Pelman gave a casual wave of the hand. "Oh, whatever one might say about our Rosa's morals, no one can deny she is a devoted daughter. So, you do not have her here?" He peered at Bear as if evidence of Miss Neatham's whereabouts might be written on his forehead.

"On our brief acquaintance, I thought her a most ladylike and demure creature."

Pelman laughed, a bark of a sound. "Yes, she gives that impression. She is a tigress in bed, though, I can tell you. The baron taught her some famous tricks. Of course, he was used to London paramours."

Courtesy or no courtesy, Pelman was an inch from being hurled into the nearest puddle. "I am finding this conversation distasteful, Pelman. And I must say, if that hovel from which I removed Mr Neatham was the standard of accommodation you offer your mistresses, you are a cad."

The man clearly had a death wish, for he continued unperturbed, "Once Rosa decides to be reasonable, I will find her something better." He frowned. "Though if you have turned her head, I suppose she might keep being difficult. Still, you don't plan to stay, do you? She'll be mine in the end."

Over Bear's dead body, or Pelman's, which was the better idea. "Time for you to leave, Pelman."

Pelman tipped back the last of his brandy. "What? You are throwing me out?"

"It is time for you to leave. On your feet would be my preference, for I am a peaceable man." Twenty-four years of war was enough for any man. Bear would not fight unless he had to, but he was considering an exception for Pelman. Pelman must have seen the urge to murder in Bear's eyes, because he stopped grumbling, led the way back toward the front door, but suddenly stopped and hurled open the door to the parlour.

Bear came up behind his shoulder. A quick glance showed a blanket draped casually over the couch where Mr Neatham lay asleep, hiding the man from view. Rosa had also removed her work-basket and herself. The room, at least from the door, appeared empty.

Bear let his anger colour his voice. "Pelman, are you calling me a liar to my face? For I cannot imagine any other reason for you to open doors in my house. Let me make this perfectly clear. Miss Neatham is not my mistress. Furthermore, I do not believe she is, or has been, your mistress, and if you continue to insult her, I will feel impelled to introduce your teeth to the back of your throat."

Pelman backed away toward the escape route of the front door, picking up his rain cape and hat as he passed. "Now, now. No need for violence."

"I hope not, for I am a peaceable man."

Once he reached the safety of the front path, Pelman turned back. "She is not worth it, you know, whatever she may have told you. Acts respectable, but everyone knows the aunt who ran off with a soldier to become a light skirt in London was really her mother, and the one she claimed as her mother was the baron's mistress. A role she took up herself when Neatham's wife died. I attended school with the current Lord Hurley, and he told me everything."

Bear took a deep breath until the red faded from his vision. *Pounding the man into the paving stones would not solve anything.* "Pelman, you have done me several services. I have paid you for the information about the hall that you sent before I came. I have yet to pay you for securing this cottage for me, and for ensuring it was stocked with fresh food. Wait there and I will fetch the money for that now, and we shall part ways." Bear closed the front door to prevent Pelman from re-entering and fetched his billfold from the study.

When he emerged from the house, Pelman stood in the same place, as if frozen, his jaw slightly dropped. He shook his head in slow disbelief. "You are... You are dismissing me as your agent? Over Rosa Neatham?"

Bear raised his eyebrows. "I cannot dismiss you, because I did not appoint you. Your old school friend recommended I use you for a couple of tasks. Here. Ten pounds should cover it."

"I cannot believe you are dismissing me over a light skirt."

Pelman took the money and tucked it inside his coat, then glared at Bear. "She must really have you gulled."

"Goodbye, Pelman."

"I rode all the way out here to check that you were well, just to find that you are taking that whore's part against..."

Bear took a threatening step forward and Pelman scurried for the gate. *Obnoxious worm.*

By the time Mr Gavenor returned from seeing Mr Pelman from the premises, Rosa had restored the parlour to rights. Thank goodness, Father had slept through the whole incident. He was sleeping more these days, which she appreciated on the one hand, and worried about on the other.

"Where were you hiding?" Mr Gavenor asked with that amused quirk of the lips.

"Under the table," she admitted, "with my work basket. And a very tight fit it was, too."

"That was quick thinking," he said.

To distract herself from the pleasure his approval gave her, she asked, "What did Mr Pelman want?"

"To find out whether I am bedding you," he said bluntly.

Rosa felt herself turn scarlet, though with temper or embarrassment, she could hardly say. "The horrid cur! He thinks everyone is of the same stamp as him, the lecherous, arrogant, nasty fool. I am sorry to bring such insult upon you, Mr Gavenor."

The amused twinkle reappeared. "Men do not consider themselves insulted if accused of attracting the attention of a pretty woman, Miss Neatham." Then, with a frown, "I reproved him for the insult to you, however."

"He asked me himself, you know," Rosa admitted. "Starting when he first visited with the new baron, after Lord Hurley died. At first, I thought he was courting me. He was, I suppose, but not with marriage in mind. When he made his proposition, he was not pleased I said 'no.'"

"The cad," Mr Gavenor said. "Has he been bothering you ever since?"

"Not all the time. He took up with Penny Able, and then there was a widow who came here to live for several years. But after Father's fall, he has kept returning. He refuses to believe I would rather die than be his mistress."

Mr Gavenor's lips twitched again. "He is a remarkably obtuse man. He refused to believe I was dismissing him as my agent."

"You dismissed him? Why?"

Both blond eyebrows jutted toward his hairline. "You can ask? He has been persecuting you, Miss Neatham, and using me as an excuse for it. It is intolerable."

Ah. When Mr Pelman involved Mr Gavenor in his campaign against Rosa, he ruffled Mr Gavenor's male pride. Rosa had seen pride drive both Lord Hurley and her father. Men were odd creatures. "He means to drive me into a corner where I have no choice," she said, "and I cannot understand it. Why would a man want a mistress who hates him?"

"He is too puffed up in his own conceit to believe you hate him," Mr Gavenor said.

"He will have to accept it." Rosa nodded firmly, determined to find some way to survive that did not include prostituting herself to her persecutor. "Even if I am driven to selling myself so I can look after my father, it will never be to Mr Pelman. Although, I have not the first idea how one goes about seeking a buyer for such a service."

She gasped. "Oh dear. I cannot believe I said that out loud." She hoped Mr Gavenor would not think she was asking him... Her cheeks burned with such heat she could barely look at the man.

This time, the quirk turned into a full grin, but Mr Gavenor just said kindly, "We will pretend it unsaid, then, shall we?"

"Please. I feel such a fool. Dinner must be nearly ready, Mr Gavenor. Shall we see?"

CHAPTER 11

After dinner, Bear sighed over his notes, which had become wet and then smudged in his pocket. Miss Neatham twisted her head to look at the ledger into which he was transcribing his findings.

"You have a neat hand," she observed.

"It was beaten into me at school," he told her. "Horrid place. I was never more pleased than when my mother decided to buy me into the military."

"You went straight into the army from school?"

He nodded. He had been young for an ensign, but his size meant people took him for older. And he grew up soon enough, especially after a few battles. "I was twenty-four years a soldier, Miss Neatham."

"Twenty-four years? But you cannot be forty, yet!"

Bear resisted preening at her assessment of his age. "Forty-two, and I joined up when I was sixteen."

She looked at him aghast. "Your mother sent you into the army when you were sixteen? What did your father say?"

"He had always intended me for the army. My mother fulfilled his wishes." He tried for a joke, "I daresay she would have handed me over after my father's funeral if they had taken eight-year-olds."

Her eyes widened with horror before she looked down at her ever-present sewing. "But you were pleased, you say." She sounded doubtful.

"Yes. The army suited me, especially when I was young. And I suited it." Until he got sick of the endless futility.

She made no comment.

Bear contemplated his notes, trying to remember whether the figure obscured by a water stain had been 54 or 64. He would have to measure that wall again. He closed the ledger, made a note of the measurements he would have to repeat, and tossed the water-damaged notes into the fire.

Miss Neatham frowned at her sewing.

"It was for the best," Bear told her. "My mother could not stand the sight of me, and I was glad to get away, even to school."

"But she must have been proud of your army record," Miss Neatham prompted. "Mrs Raby said you were a war hero; one of Lion's Zoo, she told me, which she says is a very fine thing, though I did not precisely understand it. A group of officers? And you worked for the Duke himself?"

"A silly name," Bear grumbled. "Our colonel was baptized Lionel and has a lion on his family crest. He has been called 'Lion' since he was a small boy, and I have been 'Bear' for as long. We also had a Fox and a Cat. After that, every officer who joined us had the name of a beast foisted on him. We acquired a Bull, a Tiger and a Snake. Even a Wyvern and a Centaur."

Her face came alive with interest, and she leaned forward as if to hear better, her sewing disregarded in her lap. "A very good rider, I take it."

"The best. He was younger than I when he joined as a drummer boy, but we found he could ride anything even vaguely horse-like. Broken or unbroken."

He told her about the day he and Fox first saw Cen catch a crazed horse in the aftermath of a battle, calm it, treat its wounds, and bring it back to its owner. That story led to another, and then another, and they were both surprised when Mr Neatham woke, demanded a chamber pot, and they realized how late it was.

"Thank you," Miss Neatham said before she went off to bed. "I do not know when I have more enjoyed an evening."

"I am afraid I spent the whole evening talking about myself," Bear said. Her apparent interest had spurred him on. So different from the bored debutantes he had briefly considered courting last Season. They asked for his stories, but their eyes glazed over within minutes, and he soon learned that any conversation must include the latest fashions or gossip in order to engage their attention.

"It was wonderful," Miss Neatham replied. "I have never been out of this village, Mr Gavenor; barely outside the grounds of Thorne Hall. Someone like you, who has travelled the world and seen so much—why, your stories are better than a book!"

That, from the daughter of a librarian, Bear mused as he helped Mr Neatham prepare for bed, was great praise indeed.

CHAPTER 12

The rain continued for days, turning tumbling streams into rivers, every path and lane into a tumbling stream, and every bank into a series of waterfalls. At last, a day dawned that was crisp and clear. A few white clouds scudded high in the sky.

Bear walked as far as he could toward the village, to find that the bridge was gone. They would be cut off from the direct route to the Mersey and across it to Liverpool until the bridge was rebuilt, or until the river dropped back into a fordable stream. Presumably, the local landowners would be approached to fund the replacement bridge, and Bear didn't mind contributing at all. In fact, he'd do his best to persuade them of the need for a stronger, higher bridge. His industrialist buyers wouldn't want a country home where the weather might isolate them from their enterprises.

He spent most of the day at the hall, making extensive notes about what needed to be torn down, what must be replaced, what could be repaired, and what would do with a minimum of refurbishment. He was tired but satisfied when he returned home to Rose Cottage and found an appetizing dinner waiting for him, and Rosa and her father as company to share it with. A man could get used to this.

The idea that had been evolving in the back of his mind crystallized. Why shouldn't he get used to it? He needed, or, at least, wanted a wife, and Rosa needed a husband; someone to protect her from nuisances like Pelman, and give her status in the community.

He would have to think through the idea, for there must be some substance to the accusations against her. Not as much as Pelman and his sister made out, undoubtedly, but some seed of scandal from which the rest of the ugly plant had grown.

What would scandal matter, though, when they left this place, and she was Rosa Gavenor, not Rosabel Neatham? Whatever she had been forced to by her poverty, Rosa had the training and instincts of a lady, and if she were not a complete innocent, then neither was he. She could be the hostess he needed when he had to charm potential clients, and she was certainly young enough to breed an heir for Aunt Clara.

Not to mention that his male parts ached to engage with her in the activity required to produce such an heir. For a moment, Pelman's words 'a tigress in bed' reverberated in his loins, but he'd not credit a word the man said. However much he might hope that part, at least, of the allegations proved to be true.

He thanked Rosa for the meal and took his brandy through to his study while she made her way up to bed, reminding himself sternly that she had given him no encouragement to follow her, and she was, in some sort, under his protection. He was not the kind of cowardly scoundrel who would proposition a woman with no power to refuse him.

Not like Pelman. What a swine the man was.

He sat cradling his brandy glass, sipping occasionally, and running ideas through his mind as he thought about the future.

Jeffreys turned up the next day. Bear was at Thorne Hall again, continuing his careful documentation of his new assets and liabilities.

"Mr Gavenor, sir," his manservant greeted him. "The lady at the cottage said I would find you here."

"Jeffreys! Good to see you, man. I didn't expect you until they bridged the river again."

Jeffreys explained that he had travelled through Cheshire and along the Wirral Peninsula's south coast, rather than crossing into Lancashire and taking the ferry across the Mersey from Liverpool, as Bear had.

"Shorter, and it suited the horses, sir. Miss Neatham said I won't find stabling fit for them here, but that the farmer just back along the road might board them for us. A five-minute walk, that'd be, sir, so no problem. Oh. And she said that she would have a meal on the table at noon, should you wish for one. Not to worry if you preferred to work on, for she could send some bread and cheese now she had someone to send. That would be me, once I have placed the horses."

Jeffreys gave Bear a half salute and turned to go, but Bear put his writing materials and measures into his satchel and said, "I'll walk back with you now, Jeffreys."

They made their way through the overgrown park toward Rose Cottage.

"So, you didn't go through the village?" Bear asked. "Good. I have a slightly odd request, which concerns the honour of the lady. She hurt her ankle, you see, and was unable to return to the village. Although I fetched her father, the village might not think him an adequate chaperon since he is— since his mind is failing. Especially if they know the three of us have been alone in the house."

"I see, sir," Jeffreys replied with a quick sideways glance. "I take it I arrived not long after you, then, and have been here all along."

Bear nodded. "Good man, Jeffreys. Though the farmer will know."

"The horses were turned out in the garden," Jeffreys ventured. "No good for long term, but enough for a few nights, with that old shed for cover for their feed and shelter in the worst of the storm."

"Good enough." Yes, that would do. It would not still all the gossip, but it would help. His other idea might serve for the rest. He would need to think about it a bit more and talk to Miss Neatham.

"Not that I will explain unless I am asked," Jeffreys added.

"I leave it in your capable hands."

Rosa was ejected from the kitchen after lunch. Mr Gavenor's man, Jeffreys, insisted that he would do the dishes. Very well, then, she would take advantage of the fine weather and her increasing mobility to hobble down the path and see how her hens fared. Mr Gavenor had reported that the bantam's chicks had hatched but was unable to answer her questions about their colours or even their number.

She opened the wicker door to let them scratch in the garden, and was seated on an upturned bucket, one warm chick cupped in her hand, counting the others and laughing at their antics, when Mr Gavenor joined her.

"Miss Neatham. I thought to redeem myself by examining these wee bits of fluff more closely, and here you are before me."

"We have seven," Rosa told him proudly, offering him the one she held. "Which, from nine eggs, is a good result, I assure you. More, and the bantam would have trouble covering them while they are still young and vulnerable. The eggs were from the larger hens, you see, so the chicks will outgrow their mother quite quickly. Now, we just need to wait to see how many are hens and how many cocks. I get a good price for my hens." She faltered. "Or you will, now."

Mr Gavenor pursed his lips in a quick grimace. "As to that, Miss Neatham, the hens are yours, and you must do with them as you will." He scratched the little chick on its throat and breast with one gentle finger, causing it to stretch its neck ecstatically. She waited for whatever else he had to say.

"I have a proposition for you."

Rosa froze. She had not expected that. He had always treated her with such courtesy and respect. Disappointment in him warred with relief that she had a way out of the trap Pelman was weaving around her, and a certain anticipation. What would it be like? It would involve intimate touching; she knew enough to understand that. Where even the thought of Pelman taking such liberties set her skin crawling, Mr Gavenor had quite a different effect, warming her in places about which ladies were not meant to think.

She would accept, of course, and hope she did not disappoint him, but he was still talking, not noticing her distraction.

"You and your father should never have been forced to leave Rose Cottage. I would like you to continue to regard it as your home. And I would like to remain as your boarder, if you would not mind. It is very convenient to Thorne Hall, which means I can keep a close eye on the works once they start."

She must be staring like a stunned rabbit as she scrambled to rearrange her thoughts. *Boarder. Not lover.*

"You have already taken over the housekeeping duties of a landlady, and, of course, I will owe you for the stores I have used while I have been in residence. But I am sure we can work out those financial details if you think you might be willing to accept the position. What do you say?"

Close your mouth, Rosa. Think. Then answer the question. "I— But— But Mr Gavenor, Rose Cottage belongs to you. I should be paying a rental, not charging you board."

"We can work out a rental and deduct it from the board payment. But the business about the goats was disgraceful." His voice turned stern. "You will oblige me, Miss Neatham, by going through the house and grounds and making a comprehensive list of all of the items and animals that belong with the cottage, and those that belong to you and Mr Neatham."

A reprieve for as long as the building work lasted, and after that while the money held out. Surely, time enough to find another way to support her father. One that did not require her to abandon her morals. "I— I don't know what to say."

Mr Gavenor gifted her with a boyish grin, his eyes dancing. "Say 'yes, Mr Gavenor.'"

After he'd received the reply he wanted and left for the Hall, she sat for a long time, watching the chicks and thinking about Mr Gavenor's kindness. The gentle hands that had so carefully handled the chick would not now be touching her.

Rosabel Neatham, you should be ashamed of yourself, she admonished, trying to dismiss vaguely formed ideas of what those hands might do. Of course, a man of his experience would not want a dried-up old spinster who had none. She should be thanking God for her deliverance, not sitting here in the garden mooning over might-have-beens.

A list. Mr Gavenor had asked for a list. She stood with sudden decision, causing the chicks to scurry for the protection of the bantam mother. She would keep herself busy, and these indecent thoughts would fade away.

CHAPTER 13

Bear stepped out of the terrace door in Thorne Hall's undamaged wing just as a buggy approached the large carriage circle in front of the hall. The driver was the village rector, Dr Whitlow. Bear hurried down to meet him.

"Good day, Dr Whitlow. I take it the bridge is up again?" And the rector out already, seeing to the care of souls. Bear would lay odds this visit had been prompted by the village gossips. *What would the rector demand? Miss Neatham out on her ear?* Bear would see about that.

"Yes, indeed, Mr Gavenor. A temporary bridge, and the squire is collecting subscriptions for a more permanent construction. I dare say he will be calling on you, sir."

Bear nodded. "If you see him before I do, please let him know that I am happy to support the project."

The rector nodded, then looked around. "You have your work cut out for you, Mr Gavenor, if you are to bring Thorne Hall back to its former condition."

"I have been pleasantly surprised," Bear said. Perhaps he was wrong about the rector's errand. "My seller considered it a wreck, fit only for demolition, and certainly the library wing will have to go.

The stables, too, though I have just been considering whether they can be made sturdy enough to provide sleeping space for my work crew during the rebuild. The rest, we can salvage. Would you like to take a look around?"

The rector nodded and descended from the buggy. Once the horse had been tethered in the shade, close to a trough of water, Bear led the way back toward the house, but the rector stopped after a few paces, a deep frown wrinkling his brows and eyes.

"You may wish to rescind your hospitality when you hear what I have to say, Mr Gavenor."

Now they would have at it.

"I have come to discharge an unpleasant duty," Dr Whitlow said.

"Then you had better get it over with, Rector," Bear advised. "Unpleasant duties do not improve on keeping."

Dr Whitlow swallowed, then lifted his chin, jutting it slightly. "It is about Rosabel Neatham, sir."

"I see." Bear offered no more. *Let the man dig his own hole.*

The chin jutted still further. "I have been given to understand, sir, that she is living with you in Rose Cottage without benefit of matrimony."

That was clear enough, and something Bear could answer honestly and directly. "You have been given to understand a lie, rector, if by that you mean that Miss Neatham and I have been intimate."

Dr Whitlow reared his head and raised his eyebrows. "I mean that Rosabel Neatham is known to be your mistress."

Bear kept his face impassive and his voice calm. *No point in shooting the messenger.* "Miss Neatham is not my mistress, and anyone who has told you differently is a liar."

"Do you deny that the woman is living in Rose Cottage, under your protection?" The rector's reply sounded more like a question than an accusation, which helped Bear to keep his answer calm and factual.

"Miss Neatham and her father live in Rose Cottage, yes, as they have for a number of years. Miss Neatham has been kind enough to rent me and my valet a room so I will be close to Thorne Hall, which I plan to restore."

The rector frowned. "But I am told that you own Rose Cottage, and that Miss Neatham was ejected to make way for you, at your instructions, but later insinuated her way into your household."

Bear had heard enough. "That lying cur Pelman is your informant, I take it. I did not know of Miss Neatham's existence, nor that the cottage was occupied. Pelman did, indeed, take advantage of my request for accommodation in order to remove the lady and her elderly, crippled father from their home, to place them in a hovel in Sunrise Lane." He narrowed his eyes. "You might take the measure of the man who makes these accusations from the fact he promised to house them more suitably if Miss Neatham would consent to be his mistress."

The rector paled as he rubbed his chin, then rallied. "It was both Mr and Miss Pelman. Yes, and not them alone, I can assure you, Mr Gavenor. Mr Pelman is a respected member of our community, and his sister is a stalwart of the parish. The things they have told me about Miss Neatham and the late Lord Hurley—I was not rector here at that time, but the squire supports their story, and he is a cousin of Miss Neatham's, through the mother, who was herself a scandal in the parish in her time." He frowned again, a note of doubt entering his voice. "Or so I have been told."

A cousin? Miss Neatham had not mentioned the relationship.

"The Pelmans did not live in the parish when Lord Hurley was alive, so any stories they have must have come from someone else. Rector, I prefer direct evidence, and in this case, I am suspicious about the motives of those spreading the stories."

Dr Whitlow looked concerned, which was a good step better than righteous.

Bear continued, "I have found Miss Neatham to be all that is ladylike. I would need evidence of any wrongdoing, Rector, and I have so far heard nothing but spite, gossip, and hearsay. As for cousins, family feuds can be terrible things. I would need to know a lot more."

The rector considered this, and then nodded. He had begun to walk again, his hands now clasped behind him. Bear kept pace as the man began, "I have been told—mind you, I was not here—that the late Mrs Neatham and her younger sister grew up at Threxton Grange."

Daughters of the squire? Near relatives, in any case.

"The two girls were nieces of the squire of that time, father to the current squire's mother. The current squire's father was a distant relative who married his predecessor's daughter when he inherited, as is only proper, though I have heard he was betrothed to the late Mrs Neatham before the scandal. But I am telling the story out of order." The rector stopped and bowed an apology.

"The old squire had no sons, you see. Just the one daughter, and the other two little girls who were the offspring of his sister. He doted on his nieces, particularly Lillibelle, the younger. The villagers tell me that the older niece, Rosemary, was pretty as a picture, but Lillibelle was a true beauty. Yes, and she knew it, by all accounts. Her niece is just her image. Indeed, many people believe... But I am leaping ahead again."

Bear could guess what came next. The village beauty and the passing rake. It was a story old as time. He began walking, and the rector fell into step beside him.

"It was the usual story, of course," the rector continued. "A spoilt beauty. A military man who made who-knew-what promises. A runaway marriage that proved to be not a marriage at all, and another young woman lost to the great sewer of London. The squire took an apoplexy. He did not die for a year, but he was never the same and his heir came to live with them and to take over the reins." Dr Whitlow sighed, though whether for the lost girl or the dead squire, Bear couldn't tell.

"So, how did the younger daughter's disgrace affect the older sister?" Bear asked.

"Ah, that is an interesting question. There was a breach; on that, all are agreed." The rector slipped back into storytelling mode, "If the heir had indeed been betrothed to Rosemary, someone broke the engagement, for the next thing the village knew, banns were being read for her and the librarian at Thorne Hall, Mr Neatham, who was at least a decade older than the bride, and had not—to anyone's knowledge—previously shown an interest, though he had been teaching French to all three girls."

"And the squire's heir—whose son is now squire himself — did not take the new betrothal well?"

The rector nodded thoughtfully. "You make a good point. Even the squire himself dates the breach in the family back to Rosemary's marriage. They did not approve. Rosemary was of age, and the squire's family could not stop the wedding, but the families have ignored one another ever since."

The rector frowned again, clearly considering the stories he had heard. "I am told Neatham and Hurley were both solicitous of the new Mrs Neatham, especially when she was found to be with child. They took her to Liverpool for her lying in, and many think that the baby she brought home was Lillibelle's, and not hers, at all. Certainly, Rosabel was the only child the Neathams produced."

They reached the stable yard as the rector talked, and Bear stood looking up at the damaged weathervane crowning the highest point of the roof.

Dr Whitlow followed his gaze. "So that is Miss Neatham's history, Mr Gavenor, and it is, as you say, mostly old stories—with the support of the squire and his mother, mind you, whom I am inclined to believe."

What a load of old codswallop. Miss Neatham had been made miserable as a result of such smoke and mirrors? Bear allowed an edge to enter his tone, "I have not met the squire or his mother, but I have met Miss Neatham. I have no intention of condemning her on the basis of a story that might be no more than a family falling out plus an ancient scandal."

"She does behave in a most acceptable manner," the rector conceded, "but what about the stories she was the mistress of Lord Hurley himself?"

Bear thought it all too likely. From what the current Lord Hurley said, the man was a satyr, a connoisseur not just of rare books but of tidbits to sate the physical appetites. A beautiful child with a neglectful father growing up in his very house? Still, he didn't see why anyone should blame her for it, especially without proof. He'd cast doubt on the story if he could. "A man of her father's age, I believe?"

"Perhaps a trifle older," the rector admitted.

Bear confined himself to one lifted eyebrow, letting Dr Whitlow do his own thinking.

"He was a wealthy man, Mr Gavenor," the rector pointed out. "Women think of such things when accepting a protector."

Bear presented his best defence of Miss Neatham's essential innocence, "Miss Neatham has been living in this village in dire poverty, Dr Whitlow. Does that sound like a calculating woman to you?" He pressed his point, "Tell me. When did the stories about Miss Neatham and Lord Hurley first surface? During the baron's lifetime?"

"I would not know, sir. As I said, I arrived not long after the baron died."

"When such rumours would have been aired, I would think. Were they?" If the rumours predated the Pelmans' arrival, they were more likely to be true.

Dr Whitlow shook his head. "Not in my presence. It is only in the last two years that I have been told… You understand, this does not mean the rumours had not been rife for years beforehand. Often, the rector is the last to know."

Having met the Pelmans, Bear could think of another credible explanation. "Or you didn't hear because those who wanted to spread rumours waited for Miss Neatham's father, her only protector, to become crippled in mind and body before they launched their attack."

Dr Whitlow was horrified. "What you suggest is outrageous, sir. Why, that would be malice beyond my understanding. Do you really think… I cannot believe it."

"I can," Bear said, "very readily."

"But this is terrible." Dr Whitlow took a hasty step as if he would abandon the field and hurry back to his buggy. "You say that Miss Neatham…? And Pelman really tried to force her to be his mistress?"

"He told me so himself."

"I am shocked. I will need to consider this, Mr Gavenor." The rector contemplated the ruin before him, though Bear rather thought he was seeing the gossipers of the village, instead. "If the lady is innocent, then my errand becomes more urgent." His voice became stern. "The whole village is preparing to shun Miss Neatham. While I accept your word as a gentleman that relations between you have been chaste, she has been compromised beyond any hope of recovery, except through marriage. I trust you know your duty, Mr Gavenor."

Bear had won more than he'd hoped and would be satisfied. The rector was a fair-minded man and would not condemn Miss Neatham without better evidence than old family gossip. "Whatever evil minds might think, Miss Neatham has not been compromised. She has been chaperoned throughout her stay, and no one shall attempt to force her hand. Do you hear me, Rector? No one. But yes. I know my duty, and if Miss Neatham would consent to marry me, I would consider myself greatly privileged." That should give the rector enough ammunition for some undoubtedly difficult conversations with the village's most influential residents.

The rector looked doubtfully at Bear. "We understand one another then."

"I think we do. You have your task, Rector, and I have mine."

CHAPTER 14

That afternoon, Rosa watched Mr Gavenor descend from the rector's buggy. She couldn't believe that the rector's news had been good, and prepared for further disappointment.

Mr Gavenor joined her in the parlour as soon as he had changed for dinner. Thankfully, they were alone, for Father had a slight cough and asked to stay in bed, and Jeffreys had insisted that she allow him to tend to the invalid while she joined Mr Gavenor.

Mr Gavenor didn't keep her waiting, opening the topic as soon as they had finished serving themselves. "Miss Neatham, the rector came out to Thorne Hall today. He wanted to tell me that the village has been talking."

"I expected it." Rosa was proud that her voice did not shake. "When do you wish us to move out? I can put weight on my ankle again."

"I do not wish you to move out," Mr Gavenor replied. He put down his cutlery and met Rosa's eyes, his own serious. "I will move into the village for a couple of weeks."

"But your work…" Rosa didn't understand. "A couple of weeks… What can you mean?"

Mr Gavenor looked down at his plate, then ran his hand

through his hair, a gesture of frustration. "I am doing this wrong. Look, Miss Neatham." He reached across the corner of the table and took her hand. "Rosabel. Would you do me the very great honour of becoming my wife?"

"Your wife?" Rosa frowned. He could not be proposing, surely?

"It will protect you and your father, and it would suit me very well, too," Mr Gavenor said, hurrying on before she could find a more coherent response. "A wife would be a great benefit to me, as these past few days have demonstrated. Someone to look after my house and make it into a home. I have never been more comfortable. I like having you around."

"But—"

"And it isn't just that. You would be an asset in my business. I need to entertain from time to time, and you would show to advantage among the people with whom I deal. You are a lady to the fingertips, Rosa, and the people who buy my houses would like that."

Rosa blinked, her mind a scramble.

"Also, I need a child. A daughter would be best, because my great aunt's property must be left to a girl, but we could try again if we had a son, and an heir would be rather nice, I think. I had thought of adopting, but a child needs a mother, and that means a wife."

The yearning for a child hit her in the gut, and the pain allowed her to make the first of her many objections. "But…I am thirty-six."

Mr Gavenor dismissed her age with an airy wave. "I am forty-two. Which means we are both still capable of having a child."

"Surely, there are younger women with better connections…"

He shook his head, a firm negative. "I don't want them. Silly ninnies. No conversation." His voice softened, "I like you, Rosa. I like spending time with you."

What did one say to such a thing? Rosa had no experience with compliments. "Thank you."

Mr Gavenor's brows drew together. "I don't want… Rosa, you deserve to have choices, and you won't have them in this village. If you won't marry me, will you let me find you and your father a house somewhere away from here, where you can live without your aunt's history following you?"

Rosa flinched. Her mother used to talk about her aunt, how she had been disappointed by a man and had died. Her father refused to allow the woman to be discussed, and Rosa had guessed the story was more sordid than her mother had been willing to tell a child. "You know about my aunt?"

"The rector told me," Mr Gavenor said.

"And you still want to marry me?"

He nodded firmly. "You are not your aunt, and very few families lack a skeleton or two in their closet." A second hand came to join the first; he enfolded her small hand in his large ones. "Marry me, Rosa. I will try to be a good husband."

It made no sense. Surely a man like him—wealthy and a war hero—did not need to marry an ageing spinster of no particular family from a remote corner of Cheshire. "You could find a better wife."

"I've tried. One Marriage Mart was enough." He tried for pathos, watching her from under his brows to see if she was sympathetic. "I'm never going back. If you won't have me, I'll dwindle into a lonely old man."

"I cannot help but feel that I benefit most from this arrangement." She was considering it. She was really considering marriage to Mr Gavenor. *Who would have thought?*

"The benefits go both ways. You get a home and respectability. I get a home and all the things we have listed."

"We have no guarantee I am fertile," she warned.

He seemed to think he had won, for his grin became smug. "That would be true no matter who I married."

"I need to think. May I give you my answer tomorrow?" Surely by tomorrow he would have changed his mind. For if he did not, the answer must be yes. For her father's sake, if for no other reason; and there were a multitude of other reasons.

In the early dawn, when she served him coffee and a plate loaded with food to fuel his morning's work, he did not pester her for a decision, but he returned early for lunch, driven home by a heavy shower.

"Have you had enough time to think, Miss Neatham?" he asked, as he entered the kitchen door and interrupted her bread making.

"Yes, Mr Gavenor."

He stripped off his rainwear and advanced on her with hands outstretched. "Yes, you have had time to think? Or yes, you will marry me?"

Rosa blushed, and allowed him to capture her hands.

"Yes, I will marry you, Mr Gavenor."

He bent from his great height and brushed her lips with his. "Then you had better call me Bear, as my friends do. Or Hugh, if you prefer. My great aunt used to call me Hugh."

"Hugh, then. Thank you, Hugh. I shall try to be a good wife."

He kissed her again, another butterfly touch of the lips, then put his hands on her waist and lifted her to sit on the dresser. Now her face was level with his.

"That is better," he murmured against her mouth. Then his lips met hers again, not a mere brush this time, but a gentle and inexorable advance, setting her lips tingling and taking her breath. His hands slid behind her, pulling her against his chest, so he stood between her open knees, his body pressed tightly to hers.

No, just one hand hugged her, for the other came up behind her head, and tipped it slightly, holding it in place as his lips moved against hers and his tongue swept the seam of her shut mouth once, twice, and again. He hummed with satisfaction when she parted her lips a little, letting his tongue dart inside, and her whole body hummed with pleasure.

Pelman had subjected her to a kiss once; an awkward, embarrassing thing, with her twisting to escape and him boxing her into a corner and pawing her body while he slobbered on her face. The new Lord Hurley, who had also propositioned her when he first arrived at the Hall, had respected her refusal. In fact, he had rather avoided her, and had left again not long after the will was read.

Pelman laughed when she said 'no' and waylaid her when she

was alone. It had, until now, been her only experience of the pastime, and she had not seen the appeal.

It was very different being the focus of Bear's undivided attention, the recipient of his tender passion.

She lost herself in the new feelings, grasping his shoulders to bring herself closer to his body, trying her best to imitate the movements of his mouth and tongue.

He pulled away, and rested his forehead on hers, still holding her close. "We had best stop, Rosabel. You are to be my wife, and worthy of all respect, and I have no intention of tupping you on the kitchen dresser. At least, not until we are wed."

Rosa reluctantly let him go, and he stepped back a little so he could lift her down to the floor. She was pleased to see he looked almost as dazed as she felt. "Would you call me Rosa?" she asked.

"If you wish, though Rosabel suits you. Beautiful rose. My beautiful Rosa. Much better than the ones growing outside, for your thorns do not draw blood." He still held her waist, and he leaned forward to drop a kiss on her hair. "I will move to the village this afternoon, Rosa, and will ask the rector to post the banns tomorrow."

CHAPTER 15

The timing was excellent. Bear had done all he could at Thorne Hall. Now he needed to talk to the local suppliers of building materials and labour, and prepare for the skilled work crew from Liverpool who would arrive within a week. He could better do that if he were living in the village.

He would miss Rosa, and that in itself was an excellent reason to move. This marriage was a practical business arrangement, and a fortnight to get his feelings into better order would help him remember that.

She was either a very good actress or even more innocent than he thought, her kiss enthusiastic but unpractised. The idea of tutoring her had him groaning and adjusting the fit of the moleskins he'd donned for his trip to the village.

She was waiting to see him off, looking as bereft as he felt. "I will hire a maid and a cook, Rosa, and send them out to you," he promised, then had to argue it was his right as her betrothed to pay for the servants he would certainly insist on having once they were wed.

"The cook is as much for the business as for the household, since

I usually feed the gang's foreman several times a week during a project."

"Making enough for one more at the table is hardly work at all," Rosa retorted.

In fighting her corner, she had recovered her poise. Something to remember. If this wife he had determined to take was unsettled, making her cross would help drive away the shadows.

"I'm sending them, Rosa," he said firmly. "You have enough to do with your father to care for, and I won't have you making yourself sick."

She still frowned, but she nodded. "You have made up your mind, and I must obey," she groused.

Not a good loser, his Rosa. Bear suppressed a smile and said peaceably, "In this, I will have my way. On other occasions, it will be your turn."

Rosa gave a sheepish smile. "I am being silly, am I not? Very well, Hugh. Send your servants. I suppose I will have to get used again to being always under someone's eye."

How quiet a life she must have led, Bear reflected as he and Jeffreys drove away toward the village. She'd been without servants, caring for her father on her own, for the six years since Lord Hurley died. As far as he could tell, she had little to do with the neighbours. For six years, it had been only her and her father, and he absent in his own mind. No wonder she was so self-contained.

He would be changing all of that. He hoped she would find it a change for the better.

In the village, Bear sent Jeffreys to secure rooms at the inn and to see to the horses while he visited the Rectory.

"Mr Gavenor," the rector said when he was announced, "you are speedy about your business, sir."

"To some effect, I am pleased to say." Bear took the offered seat.

"Miss Neatham has done me the honour of consenting to be my bride. We would like the banns called, Dr Whitlow."

"Immediately? Starting at tomorrow's service? Certainly, Mr Gavenor. May I say how pleased I am? I wish you both very happy."

"Yes, immediately, and with the wedding as soon as possible." It would be at least two weeks; a time that stretched before Bear like eons. Not that he didn't have plenty to do, he reminded himself.

"On Sunday after Matins, then, two weeks from tomorrow." Dr Whitlow rewarded Bear with a benign smile. "Congratulations, Mr Gavenor. I shall call on you and Miss Neatham to discuss the obligations of marriage, as is my duty, and to arrange the details of the service."

"If we set a time, I shall let Miss Neatham know and arrange to be there myself. I have moved into the village until after the wedding."

The rector inclined his head and nodded slightly. "A good idea. That, and the wedding, should serve to still some of the tongues. I regret to say that Sir Gerard and his lady wife are set in their convictions, and Miss Pelman stands with them. Mr Pelman said all that was proper, but I feel no conviction as to his sincerity."

"Mr Pelman is a snake," Bear grumbled. "Dr Whitlow, I have another mission today. I intend to hire some help for my betrothed, who has been managing all the work at Rose Cottage, including looking after her father. I would like at least two maids to live in. I want a cook, too, and a handyman to do repairs and other jobs, and perhaps a little bit of gardening. The handyman would be a casual hire, coming when my betrothed needs him." A bit of mending, a bit of gardening. The handyman would definitely not be living in; not, at least, until he and Rosa were married. The busy tongues of her enemies needed no more ammunition.

"Hmmm. The two middle Hesketh sisters might be interested. Some extra money in that household would be helpful. With the harvest so poor…perhaps the Colley son? A cook, you say? That might be a little more difficult."

Bear had intended to offer Rosa a choice, but perhaps it was better to depend on local expertise. "How should I proceed, rector?

I had thought of putting word out in the village and setting a time for interviews. I also need local labour for the work on Thorne Hall. I have a skilled team coming across from Liverpool, so the men here don't need to be experienced, but they do need to be willing and strong."

The rector considered that, his hands steepled under his chin, his fingers tapping his lips. "Write me a list, Mr Gavenor. The position, the quality and skills needed. The servants for Miss Neatham are urgent, I take it? When will you need the work crew?"

"I would prefer Miss Neatham not to be alone with the full care of her father. If we could find her at least one maid, as soon as possible, I would be easier in my mind."

The rector nodded. "Then, I suggest we visit the Heskeths. If you are satisfied, and they are willing, you will have met the immediate need. And the work crew?"

"My foreman will select and hire the men. I expect him any time in the next week. We will be taking men on for casual hire through the next six months, I imagine. Perhaps nine."

The rector looked pleased at that, and well he might. Bear would be providing wages for the rest of the dismal summer and well into winter, perhaps even spring. "When would you be free to visit the Heskeths, sir?" Bear asked.

"No time like the present." The rector stood. "They live just a five-minute walk away, on a small holding near the river, and I imagine we will find them at home, in this rain. Will you excuse me while I find a hat and an umbrella, sir?"

The Heskeths, so the rector explained as they walked, had farmed here since time immemorial, owning enough land to make them prosperous in good years, though seasons like this stretched their resources.

"Two fewer mouths to feed, and the girls' wages, will help," Bear commented.

"Yes, and old Mr Hesketh lives with them yet, and is in his second childhood, so they are accustomed to the elderly."

At the farmhouse, a rambling place that looked as if successive owners had added on since before the Norman Conquest, they were ushered into a tiny but pristine parlour, where the rector presented Bear's request to Mrs Hesketh, a comfortably cushioned lady perhaps a decade older than Bear. She frowned, her fair brows drawing together over her nose.

"Mind, I don't hold with the gossip. I never saw Miss Rosa up to anything a lady shouldn't, nor her mother before her. My own mother worked at Thorne Hall before she wed, and my sister more recently." She examined Bear carefully, peering at him as if weighing the risk of her next words. "I do not wish to offend, sir, but I'll not have my girls going into a house of sin, Mr Gavenor, and the whole world knows that you and Miss Rosa have been living there together."

Before Bear could respond, the rector spoke up, "Now Mrs Hesketh, Mr Neatham and Mr Gavenor's manservant have both been there all through, and Mr Gavenor assures me he has been merely boarding at the cottage to be close to Thorne Hall. Nothing untoward has happened. Not, at least, at Rose Cottage, though I am disappointed in the spiteful tongues of some in the village. Mr Gavenor has now moved into the village to await his wedding to Miss Neatham."

Bear thought it time to take a hand. "My betrothed had a fall several weeks ago, Mrs Hesketh, and I worry for her alone in the cottage with her frail, elderly father to care for. The rector here told me what people were saying, and I hoped to save Miss Neatham from further embarrassment. If you could see your way to permitting your girls to offer their help, I would be very grateful."

At that point, the door to the parlour opened, and three young women, each a younger copy of their mother, carried in refreshments: a tea pot, plates of scones, a tray with cups, milk and sugar.

"These are three of my daughters, Mr Gavenor," Mrs Hesketh said. "Polly, Maggie and Sukie. Polly is to be wed in a few weeks, so I'd be sending Maggie and Sukie. If Mr Hesketh agrees. If they are willing to go."

The daughters looked their questions but busied themselves laying out the tea makings.

Mrs Hesketh said, "Mr Gavenor is marrying Miss Rosa and

wants maids for Rose Cottage. Just for a few months, mind. If your Da agrees, I've a mind to let you go."

After a scone and a cup of tea, Bear and the rector walked back to the village, leaving the two excited girls packing. "They seem very confident that Hesketh will give his permission," Bear said.

The rector laughed. "Mrs Hesketh's is the approval that counts in that household. But she maintains the fiction that Hesketh is the final authority. You have your two maids, Mr Gavenor. And I have just had a thought—if you are not looking for fancy cooking, I may have someone…"

"Excellent," Bear told him. "Plain English cooking will suit me fine." *Will it suit Rosa?* he wondered, then dismissed the thought. She could hire a fancy French chef when they were closer to civilization, if that was what she wanted. Which, for some reason, reminded him of something else he wanted.

"Dr Whitlow, where can I buy a bed large enough for a man of my size?"

CHAPTER 16

As her betrothed assisted her into his chaise on Sunday morning, Rosa was conscious of two conflicting emotions. One was relief that she could leave the house for long enough to attend the church service, since the new maids had shown themselves both willing and able to look after her father in her absence. The other was trepidation. She and Bear would be the centre of attention once the banns were read for the first time. The Pelmans and the Thrextons would find something to censure, made up or real, and they had their supporters in the village.

I would feel more confident if I had something suitable to wear, she thought.

Bear had dressed for the occasion in pale breeches and stockings, a dark blue coat over an embroidered waistcoat with a creamy froth of lace at neck and cuff. He didn't favour the excesses they showed in the fashion magazines she sometimes saw at the village shop, but the materials were of the best quality and beautifully cut to fit his frame.

Rosa's Sunday-best gown had had more than six years of use, new clothes being a luxury the Neathams could not afford after the new Lord Hurley stopped the pension the former Lord Hurley had once paid. She had tried to keep it from dirt and harm, but six years was more than 300 Sundays, even allowing for those when she could not find anyone to sit with her father and had to miss services.

Turning the back panel to move the shiny spot, carefully mending tears, and cutting off the cuffs to replace them with a band taken from another gown could not disguise the fact that her Sunday-best would be a Monday washday gown for almost any other woman in the parish.

Next to Bear, she looked like a pauper, which was not far from the truth.

The mile to the village passed quickly, with just enough time for Bear to ask after her father, and tell her about his success in finding a gardener and to name the cook who would be coming on Wednesday. She had met the woman. Mrs Gillywether came from a local family but had married a farmer over in Lancashire. She had only recently moved back to live with her brother.

"You have the final say, Rosa," Bear assured her.

Jeffreys waited at the church gate to take the horses, and Bear handed Rosa down with as much reverence as if she were a duchess. As Rosa expected, people stared, but the bells proclaimed that Matins was about to begin, so she did not have to talk to anyone. Bear offered his arm and escorted her up the path and down the aisle. *Straight back, Rosa. Smile and nod to those who smile and nod at you. Keep walking. Pretend you are wearing silk.*

Usually, she slipped into the back, standing with the villagers. Today, Bear took her straight to the box pews at the front, to the Thorne Hall box that she used to sit in before Lord Hurley died. *Back straight, Rosa. You have every right to be here.*

From the corner of her eye, she glimpsed the squire's mother glaring at her. "Why does Lady Threxton hate us?" she had asked her mother, long ago when she was a child. "She is still cross because she thinks your aunt took something that was hers," Mama answered, which left the child Rosa not much wiser, and questions to Father or Lord Hurley were ignored or shushed. The breach between Thorne Hall and Threxton Grange just existed, with no explanation or remission.

The psalm singers led the opening hymn, and the rector began the service.

The stir when she entered the church on Bear's arm was nothing to the hum that ran around the church when the rector proclaimed from the pulpit, "I publish the banns of marriage between Hugh Richard Gavenor and Rosabel Marianne Neatham, both of this parish. This is the first time of asking. If any of you know of any cause or just impediment why these two should not be joined together in Holy Matrimony, ye are to declare it."

The dowager Lady Threxton half rose, but her son the squire, whispering urgently, persuaded her to sit again. Bear surveyed those who were whispering, his chin high, a small smile playing about the corners of his mouth. He gave a light, encouraging squeeze to Rosa's hand, and she smiled back. If he could pretend to be proud of a scarecrow like her, the least she could do was support him.

The gauntlet of comments and stares Rosa had expected to run on her way back to the chaise was not as bad as she'd expected. Several villagers presented their congratulations to Bear and their best wishes to her, slowing the couple's exit. By the time they reached the porch, where the rector waited to greet them while much of the parish watched, the Pelmans and Thrextons had left the church and the churchyard.

"That wasn't so bad, was it?" Bear asked as they drove away from the village. "You were so tense when we arrived, I felt I was leading you to your execution." His grin suggested that he thought his remark funny.

"I thought Lady Threxton was going to object to the banns," Rosa said.

She fell silent as Bear negotiated the slope down to the temporary bridge and up the other side. Back when they could afford a gig and horse, Father used to insist that she let him concentrate at such moments. Bear apparently had no such qualms, since he said, "Just as well her son stopped her from embarrassing herself in public."

"And us," Rosa pointed out.

He shot her a smile, even as the horses turned the sharp corner to climb back up to the road. "They can only embarrass us if we let them, Rosa. Your cousins are clinging to ancient history, when most of the main actors in that drama are dead. Pelham has taken advantage of that for his own purposes, but is heading for a fall if he thinks to continue."

"My cousins?" Rosa asked. "I don't have family apart from Father. An aunt, but she died long ago."

"You don't know?" Bear pulled the chaise to the side of the road and gave Rosa his full attention. "Rosa, the rector told me that your mother and Lady Threxton are cousins."

Rosa found that hard to believe. "That cannot be so. Surely… We have been at odds all my life, Hugh. Families do not behave like that, do they?"

Bear's eyes turned bleak. "Family members make the bitterest of enemies, Rosa. I shall tell you the story as it was told to me. You deserve to know what is behind Lady Threxton's behaviour."

CHAPTER 17

As Bear drove away from the cottage later that day, he berated himself for being every kind of idiot.

Today, he had failed Rosa not once, but several times. First, he should have realized she had nothing fit to wear to church. He'd seen the much-mended and faded gowns she wore every day, and knew she'd had little to no income for years. He'd not had time to repair the matter, since it wasn't until she paled and stiffened at the church gate that he'd even thought about her gown.

What courage she had. Head up, back straight, she'd marched into church beside him as proud as a duchess in silken splendour, and if her hand trembled on his arm, not a soul but him would ever know.

Second, he had not thought about the reaction of the villagers when they heard the banns. Not until the rector started speaking and the whole church went silent. Then came the buzz of whispers, and Lady Threxton standing. They brushed through it, thanks to the squire's intervention and the rector's support, but Bear could have bypassed the risk by simply not taking her to Matins today.

She'd impressed him again after the service, accepting good

wishes with a smile and word of thanks, and ignoring those who glowered from a distance.

Third, he'd mentioned her relationship with the squire's family, and followed up by telling her the full story. Of course, she went straight to her father when they arrived at Rose Cottage and demanded to know whether the tale was true.

At first, he had been bewildered by the question, then he took one of his erratic dives into the past, and began berating Rosa, calling her Belle.

"All you thought of was yourself, Belle. You knew better than to sneak off with a gentleman, and no true gentleman would have asked it of you. Especially since Pelman was all but betrothed to your cousin. Look where your selfishness led. You, disgraced and abandoned. Your uncle sick from the horror of it all, and your cousin so bitter against you that she has had Rosie thrown out of her home. The best thing you can do for any of us is go back to London and leave us alone."

After that, he would only say, "Go away," until Rosa gave up.

His outbreak seemed to confirm the rector's story but raised more questions. How did Pelman get into the story? Not the current Pelman, clearly, since he would have been a small child or not even born at the time of the scandal. Which sister gave birth to the baby?

"Ancient history," Rosa said, her eyes damp but her lips smiling.

Not ancient as long as it had power to affect Rosa. Bear was two weeks away from vowing to love and cherish her all his life, and he was doing a poor job of it so far.

He could fix the wardrobe; had already invited her to take a day trip to Liverpool with him on the first fine day so they could buy what she needed without the villagers commenting. He couldn't help but wonder about Lord Hurley's will. Did the old man truly make no provision for his librarian and the librarian's daughter? By all accounts, Mr Neatham had been given a pension when he retired, and Rosa had been Lord Hurley's pet, whatever the propriety of the relationship. The matter needed further investigation.

As for Rosa and her cousins, he had no idea how to fix that old breach. Rosa's naive belief that families did not feud across generations brought a grim smile. She'd never met his mother, who had despised him from birth and hated him from the day her husband and daughter died on an outing that was meant to be his. A special treat just for the two men of the household, his father had said. Bear, at eight years old, had been so proud and so excited. Until his sister Felicia spoiled her copybook and claimed that Bear had done it, so his father took Felicia instead.

"It should have been you," his mother said when they brought the news of the carriage accident. Runaway horses. No survivors.

"It was a horrible accident, Hugh," said his great aunt, when she arrived two days later. "No one's fault, unless it was your father's. Your mother is mad with grief."

Perhaps. His mother seemed sane enough, if vicious and unpleasant, but on that one point, Mother remained adamant until her death twenty years later. Her darling daughter had been killed in an accident, and it was all Bear's fault that Felicia had been there instead of Bear.

For the second reading of the banns, Rosa wore one of her new gowns. One of five, and more to come. Bear had found a dressmaker who kept a stock of gowns with the long seams sewn, and had insisted on buying all those that suited Rosa's size and colouring. Only one had been ready to collect at the end of their long day in Liverpool, and she'd worn it home on the ferry, wrapped against the wind in one of her new shawls, with one of her new hats tied firmly under her chin.

It had been a busy week.

The new cook started work the next day, which was Wednesday, and just in time, for Bear's Liverpool work crew crossed on that morning's ferry, and Bear brought the foreman to dinner.

Warned by a message, and armoured in her new gown, Rosa was able to meet Mr Caleb Redding with equanimity. With Maggie to serve and Sukie sitting with Father, she presided over the table, where the two men initially tried to keep the conversation general, but soon succumbed to discussions of the work that needed to be done to set up camp at Thorne Hall, especially since the local weather watchers were predicting a long spell of rain.

Rosa waved off their apologies, fascinated by this insight into the man she was to marry.

"That one end of the stable block is mostly sturdy enough," Mr Redding said, "and shoring up anything rickety will be easy. But plugging all the leaks? If we put our dormitory in there, we'll spend all our time fixing holes, and none on the real work."

"And if we don't," Bear argued, "we'll get even wetter when the wind gets up and the tents blow away."

They argued back and forth, until Rosa ventured, "Could you put the tents up inside the stables?"

Stunned silence greeted her question. Both men looked into some distance as they thought, then exchanged a glance and nodded.

"A brilliant suggestion, Miss Neatham," Mr Redding said, but it was Bear's proud smile that warmed her to her toes.

The other gowns arrived on Thursday, the same day as the enormous bed, which needed to be carried upstairs in pieces and assembled in the best bedchamber.

On Friday, the village dressmaker arrived to do the final fitting on the gowns sent from Liverpool, but Rosa would be crossing the Mersey again next week for the gown Bear had insisted on having made for her wedding. A gown of real silk, and Bear looked astonished when she suggested she didn't need it. Also, her second trip to Liverpool in just over a week, when before she had been there thrice in her lifetime. No, four. If the rector's story was true, Father and Mama had brought her from Liverpool as a tiny baby.

On Sunday, Rosa looked across the aisle at the squire's box, to meet the angry eyes of Lady Threxton. She took a deep breath and nodded a greeting. The old woman sniffed and turned her head away.

The rector read the banns for the second time, and Rosa relaxed, fractionally, when they passed without comment. She was safe for the rest of the service but would then have to face those of the congregation who had an opinion about her coming marriage. She was not as nervous as she had been last week. After all, nothing bad had happened then, when the news was fresh. Besides she had her new gown, and Bear, that mountain of strength and protection, was at her side.

However, Bear was carried off as soon as they left the church porch, surrounded by men who found his betrothal to the notorious Miss Neatham far less important than his call for workers to rebuild Thorne Hall.

This week, the crowd of well-wishers grew larger, and contained a number of former detractors, all people who stood to benefit if Bear chose to give them or their relatives a job or favour them with his custom.

Once again, the Pelmans and the squire's family did not look her way, as if they could imagine her out of existence, and they did not linger.

Those around her had dispersed before Bear finished with his petitioners. She thought of joining him, but a chorus of raucous laughter hinted that the all-male group might find her presence constraining. Instead, she crossed the road beyond the churchyard gate to the shade of a tree, where Jeffreys waited with the chaise and horses.

He greeted her with a nod, hurrying to the side of the chaise to let down the steps. "Did you want to take a seat to wait for Mr Gavenor, Miss Neatham?"

Not really, when who knew how long he would be? She had sat long enough on the hard seat of the Thorne Hill box pew. "I think I will just take a stroll, Jeffreys," Rosa said. "I'll walk in the direction of the bridge, just as far as the edge of the village. If Mr Gavenor is ready before I return, you can take me up on the way."

"Certainly, Miss Neatham." He retreated to the horses' heads and leaned back against the bar to which they were tethered.

Walking in the sun was possibly foolish, but the warmth was so lovely after the storms, the light cotton dress was cool, and the new hat shaded her face. She strolled, keeping to the side of the road, returning smiles as she passed the few people still about. Most of the villagers would be having their main meal before sallying forth on visits or settling to tasks that could be done on a Sunday without offending the neighbours.

Rosa had continued the habits of Thorne Hall, Lord Hurley having adopted the modern custom of dinner in the evening. The cook would have a light snack ready for her and Bear when they arrived back at Rose Cottage. The novelty of eating food she had not prepared had not worn off, and once they were private after the meal, she was fairly certain that Bear would kiss her again, as he had several times this week. The thought put a slight skip in her step.

"Pleased with yourself, are you not?" the bitter voice stopped her. Lady Threxton emerged from the shadow of the gateway into the Pelmans' back garden. "I always knew you would come to no good. An apple does not fall far from the tree."

Before she had time to think, Rosa asked the question that had burned in her mind all week, "Why do you hate me? I have never done anything to you. I know my aunt…"

She took a step back as Lady Threxton advanced on her, her face contorted with rage.

"You, your mother, your aunt. You all took what was mine. What she did killed my father, did they tell you that?"

Such virulence over so many years! Rosa made one more effort. "She left in disgrace and died. Is that not enough? They're all dead now, all the people involved. Except you and my father. Can we not let it rest?"

"Is that what they told you? That Lillibelle died?" Lady Threxton laughed, a cruel distortion of what should have been a joyful sound. "She lives, and has her hooks deeply into the Marquess of Raithby." She cackled another mirthless sound. "That is the kind of woman she is. One who tempts a married man from his vows and makes orphans of his children. The whole world knows it. Belle Clifford, she calls herself, but I saw her myself, at the Opera with her paramour. Wherever he goes, he has a place for her nearby, even on his chief estate, with the scandal columns reporting what they get up to and his wife forced to ignore what happens right under her nose."

She narrowed her eyes as she came right up to Rosa, waving her finger so close that Rosa had to back away to keep her nose from being struck.

"You, your aunt, your mother. You are all from the same bad seed. All whores." She drew back, her eyes suddenly confused. "Lillibelle? You've come back?"

Rosa had seen the same disorientation when her father began slipping away from reality. Her anger and fear receded, replaced by compassion. Her poor cousin had spent so long in the past, she was now trapped by it. Rosa hoped she had some happy memories to wander among, as Father did.

Lady Threxton whispered at her, a rage-filled hiss, "I know what you did with Pelman. You were sneaking out to see him behind my back. Just like Aunt Mary, running off with that man and getting herself killed. Two daughters for Papa to raise, and no marriage license. He should have put you both in a workhouse. He already had a daughter!"

The sound of approaching hooves and harness coincided with the younger Lady Threxton hurrying from the Pelman's garden and reaching her mother-in-law's side just as Bear pulled the carriage up beside Rosa.

"What have you said to her?" the squire's wife demanded.

"What has she said to my betrothed?" Bear corrected, dropping to land at her side and catching her elbow just in time to stop her from sagging.

She leaned into his strength, and found the fortitude to say, "She has me confused with my aunt. Best take her out of the hot sun, Lady Threxton."

"You need to sit down, Miss Neatham." Bear's eyes showed worry. "You are as white as a sheet, my dear."

She allowed Bear to help her up into the chaise, and to fuss over putting up her new parasol to shade her, while Jeffreys returned to the groom's perch at the rear.

*W*hat did the old witch say?

Bear asked no questions. Rosa needed time to compose herself, and would not, in any case, want to air her family's long-standing scandals in Jeffrey's hearing.

Rosa remained silent during the short drive, but colour had returned to her cheeks by the time Bear handed her down at Rose Cottage.

Rosa went up to check on her father, then joined Bear in the parlour, where the servants had laid out cold meats, pastries, pickled vegetables and fruits. She was calm and contained, as if the incident with Lady Threxton had not happened, but the strain showed around her eyes.

One of the Hesketh girls bustled in and out of the room with tea makings, and coffee for Bear, so private conversation would have to wait.

Instead, Bear described the work on Thorne Hall, and the new workers he planned to hire on Monday. "As you know, we've started the demolition, but it will go much faster with the extra hands." His challenge—or Caleb's rather—would be to forge teams with both skilled men and laborers, when skilled men were on foreign soil and the laborers all from Kettlesworth.

Rosa was surely just humouring him. Women didn't care where the money came from, just that it came. Or so he had always believed, but Rose listened carefully, and asked a few pertinent questions.

"Some sort of competition seems to inspire men," she said. "Could you have a weekly challenge, with a prize for the team that completes their task first? Something they would have to work together to achieve."

That could do the trick. "I like that idea, Rosa." He'd discuss it with Caleb, and they'd figure something out.

The meal finished, he invited her to take a walk to the Hall. "You haven't seen it since we started." The walk would give them time to chat, and the shrubbery between the Hall and the cottage offered plenty of cover, should he be able to persuade his shy lady that they were unobserved.

His male parts stirred at the thought, somewhat prematurely. He was determined to show proper respect by waiting for their wedding night, difficult though it was when she looked up at him with a demure smile, her face framed by her hat and its ribbon.

Arm in arm, they strolled through the gate that gave quick access to the Hall, along one of the bridle paths of the estate. First, the path from the cottage wound through a thicket of hazel, which looked as if it had been coppiced regularly for generations, and untouched for years. Another task for his list of all that was needed to make the property marketable, but currently an ideal spot for dalliance.

He looked back to check, and sure enough, he could see nothing but hazels. The same ahead and to both sides. Rosa had stopped when he did. She watched him, eyes wide, a light flush colouring her cheeks. She curled her lower lip into her mouth and ran the top teeth over it, and the salacious images that action prompted had him groaning. Did the minx have any idea what she did to him?

She certainly knew what to expect, for as he took a step toward her, she lifted her arms and cooperated in her own capture.

Several long kisses later, he lowered her gently to the path again, tortured by and revelling in her slide down his body. "Only one more week," he reminded himself, and must have spoken aloud because Rosa answered, "Just seven more days."

Bear helped Rosa with the buttons he had undone and retied her hat, which he had pushed from her head for better access to her face. Rosa had clearly been better behaved than him, since he had only to tidy his cravat and straighten his cuffs. Perhaps he could tempt her into rumpling him more on the way back.

Once they began walking again, he asked the question that had eaten at him since he'd come to Rosa's rescue earlier that day. "What did old Lady Threxton say that so upset you?"

"Oh Hugh, just the same ancient history. But… Hugh, she did not know who I was, at the end. She thought I was my aunt. She called me Lillibelle, and said I—the two of us, so Lillibelle and my mother—should have been left in the workhouse. She mentioned Pelman as Lillibelle's deceiver, which confirms the rector's story."

CHAPTER 18

Rosa couldn't tell Bear the rest of Lady Threxton's accusations. That she was Lillibelle's child. That her grandmother had also run away with a man she never married, which made Rosa's mother and aunt base born. Above all, that Lillibelle still lived, and was mistress to the Marquess of Raithby.

Such scandalous associations made her unfit to be a wife, and she should tell him the truth and release him from his promise. But, how could she? He was her salvation and her father's, and besides, Lady Threxton's mind was fading. Perhaps what she said was not true.

She let Bear whisk her into a shelter formed by two trees and kiss her thoroughly, consoling herself that the scandal was all in the past and would not touch them.

Still, the revelations preyed on her mind, particularly that her aunt, if Lillibelle was indeed her aunt, was still alive. Belle Clifford. Would it be such a terrible thing if she wrote a letter? But the post was collected at the inn, and the innkeeper's wife was a gossip. Besides, she had no address.

The thought sat at the back of her mind during a busy week. By Monday, she realized she could post the letter from Liverpool, and send it in care of the Marquess of Raithby. By Tuesday, she had already rejected two drafts. She had not yet mentioned the letter to Bear, who didn't know Lillibelle still lived, but she would have to tell him. He was escorting her to Liverpool.

She and the two maids were giving the whole house a thorough cleaning, attic to cellar, tackling all the jobs she had been unable to manage on her own. The outdoors handyman had arrived and was making order out of the parts of the garden that had been reverting to wilderness.

Bear suggested that the man cut down the rambling rose that grew up the walls of the cottage. "I don't understand why people grow roses," he grumbled. "They only flower for a short time, and they have thorns all year round."

"The roses, when they come, are worth a few scratches," Rosa retorted. "My mother used to say that thorns are not the cost of having a rose bush. The flowers are the reward for having a thorn bush." She chuckled as she remembered. "Mother used to say that she and I both had our thorns, but we were roses, for all of that."

Her betrothed laughed, and had the handyman trim ramblers a little and mulch them with straw cleaned out from the hen's coop. He also had a group of workmen remaking the shed and building an extension large enough to stable two horses and a small carriage.

Bear spent most of each day at Thorne Hall, working alongside the men, but he came to dinner each evening, bringing his foreman. Each evening he found a time and place to catch Rosa alone, for another of those toe-curling kisses.

Thursday was the day set for Rosa to return to Liverpool for the gown she would wear at her wedding. On Wednesday evening, Bear asked, "Would you mind if I do not escort you to Liverpool tomorrow, Rosa? I want to be here tomorrow when we bring down the rest of the damaged wing."

She could post her letter, now in its fifth draft, without having to explain. "Of course, Hugh. You must be at Thorne Hall for that. I can take Sukie with me for propriety."

"And Jeffreys," Bear decreed. "He will drive you to the ferry and cross with you."

. . .

"We will be some time," Rosa told Jeffreys the following day, after she had consulted with the dressmaker. "Meet us back here in two and a half hours, Jeffreys." An hour for the fitting. At least an hour to wait while they made the final adjustments, and thirty minutes for a final fitting just to be certain that the gown was perfect.

After Sukie had been dispatched with the dressmaker's maid to fetch Rosa a cup of tea, Rosa asked the dressmaker for directions to a place she could send a letter. Delighted that the post location was no more than a couple of streets away, she then put the letter out of her mind to focus on the gown.

It was the most beautiful gown Rosa had ever seen; not the lightweight, shimmering silk that Bear had initially picked, suitable only for evening, but a figured silk in a slightly heavier weave, made up as a day gown, with a modest scooped bodice and long sleeves. The dusky pink ground bore a repeated motif of stripes and flowers, and the effect was enhanced by embroidery on the cuffs and hem, using the same shapes and slightly darker colours.

The dressmaker and her seamstresses fussed over the exact fit of the bodice and the length of the cuffs. There was a pelisse, too, short waisted and in a darker rose.

She enjoyed the fitting much more than she had expected, which made the hour fly past. "We have little to do, ma'am," the dressmaker said, at last. "An hour, no more. You are welcome to wait, or if you have errands…?"

An hour. With the last of the hen money in her reticule, and a wedding present for Bear to purchase, an hour would be barely enough time. But first, the letter. The final version, although brief, addressed the essentials.

To Mrs Belle Raithby,

I am given to believe that we are related, ma'am. If this is so, then you may be the only person in the world who knows the truth of it, for Mrs Neatham, your sister, has been gone for more than twenty years, and Mr Albert Neatham is failing in his mind.

If it does not give you pain to acknowledge this voice from your past, I would be pleased to hear from you, and to have the opportunity to correspond with the last surviving member of my family.

Yours sincerely
Rosabel Marianne Neatham
Rose Cottage, Kettlesworth

Posting it was easy enough. She told Sukie to wait at the door, lined up at the rear of a short queue, and had soon handed over the princely sum of a shilling to send the letter to the Marquess of Raithby's London address.

Her remaining mission proved more difficult. Anything she saw that she liked was beyond the price she could afford, until just before the hour ended, when she found a set of four botanical paintings, framed and hung in a square.

"How much for four frames of this size?" she asked the shop assistant. By the time she had convinced him that she wanted just the frames, and bargained for a price, she was some ten minutes late returning to the dressmaker, who didn't turn a hair. Rosa, who had often been kept waiting much longer by customers, apologized and was told it was of no account.

What a thing it is to be the one spending money.

Soon, she was dressed in all her finery. The dressmaker had taken delivery of the matching slippers and gloves she and Bear had ordered last week, and the milliner who shared the same premises brought through the bonnet on which she and the dressmaker had collaborated—a soft version of the rose pink, trimmed with ribbons that picked up the colours in the gown, and with silk flowers made to mimic the embroidery.

Rosa smiled at her image. She looked almost pretty. She hoped Bear thought so.

Rosa glowed. It was the only word Bear could find to match the reality. From the moment Jeffreys had handed her down from the chaise and delivered her to Bear's waiting arm, he had been awestruck. She had gained a little weight in the weeks since he first met her, and, of course, she wore a pretty new gown, but there was more to the change than additional curves and fine feathers. She looked happy. Happy and confident. The glow suited his fairy but made Bear nervous. It would be his challenge to keep her happy, and he was by no means certain he was up to the job.

The usual Sunday service first, where their banns were read for the third time, and then the wedding ceremony. Bear had Caleb as his witness, and Rosa had asked Sukie.

Neatham, neatly dressed and carefully attended by Jeffreys and Maggie, sat in the Thorne Hall box, watching the proceedings with interest. "I am glad he married her," he said loudly, at one point. "Rosie will be pleased. She does worry about Belle."

Bear had assumed that their small household would be the entire congregation, but many of those who'd been to Matins stayed on, and Bear and Rosa exited the church to the acclaim of dozens of well-wishers.

Bear had bespoken lunch at the inn, and, on an impulse, sent Caleb on ahead to warn the innkeeper that their numbers were augmented, before inviting anyone who wished to join them.

They crowded into the inn, where the landlord put out a magnificent spread, and the village settled in to celebrate. Bear resigned himself to a couple of hours, at least, until they could get away.

They were soon separated, each surrounded by a cluster of villagers. Bear kept a weather eye on Rosa's father, but relaxed when Jeffreys and Maggie kept Neatham company and plied him with food. Bear was also conscious, at every moment, of Rosa's location in the room, as if a tether connected them through which flowed her delight in this celebration.

Each time he managed to work his way back to her, she greeted him happily. He didn't think they'd seen the last of the Pelman poison, but he did not want it to spoil this day for her.

He came up as Rosa was showing her ring to some of the farm matrons. It was a pretty thing; gold in the form of flat braids, with etched roses and a setting of five tiny roses moulded in gold, each with a diamond glinting at its centre. "It was my great aunt's," he told her, when he had an opportunity to speak quietly in her ear. "If you prefer something new…" He had sent for it the day he had proposed. Aunt Clara had worn it always, until the day she had given it to Bear. He remembered her words as if it were yesterday. *This is for the bride you choose, Hugh. My John put it on my finger on my wedding day. May it see you and your wife as happy as we were.*

Rosa's smile deepened. "This is perfect, Hugh. I will treasure it all the more because it was your aunt's."

They were called from their private moment by Caleb, who wanted to propose a toast. "To Mr and Mrs Gavenor. May this be the first of a lifetime of celebrations."

That toast was followed by another, and another. Bear noted that Rosa confined herself to sips, but even so, when he finally extracted them from their well-wishers and gave her his arm to escort her to the chaise, she leaned into him, her gait unsteady. "I feel a little odd, Bear," she whispered.

He should have realized she was unused to wine. "Just lean on me," he murmured back. "You'll be fine."

Climbing into the chaise was beyond her, which she found very funny. He lifted his giggling bride and set her on the seat, then rounded the carriage and climbed up beside her. Jeffreys stepped away from the horses' heads and Bear snapped the reins. Rosa waved her bonnet so enthusiastically that she almost lost it when it flew from her hand.

Bear, catching it, told her, "I'll just tuck this down here, Rosa, for when you need it again."

"Thank you, Bear. I am glad I stole your roses," she told him.

Minutes would see them home at Rose Cottage. At last. Would

she consent to an early night? It was still only afternoon, but it was, after all, their wedding day.

His hopes soared when she tucked herself against him, resting her head on his arm, but sank again when he glanced down to find she had fallen asleep. They were out of the village, and no observer was in sight. He dropped a kiss on her hair. So much for his plans. When he arrived at the cottage, he would indeed carry his new bride up to bed. To sleep off the wine.

CHAPTER 19

Some four hours later, Bear sat beside the large bed he'd ordered and watched his wife wake. He cupped a large glass of a pick-me-up made by Jeffreys, a recipe known only to that excellent individual.

Rosa groaned.

"Drink this, Rose. It will help with the headache."

She blinked at him, her eyes slowly focusing on his face. "We got married," she stated.

"We did."

"I do not feel well, Hugh."

Jeffreys' pick-me-up did its usual sterling service, and once Rosa had a light meal inside her, she recovered her colour and her spirits, though she was particularly quiet this evening. Conversation remained sporadic until he asked about the new garden beds the handyman had dug behind the cottage. Rosa opened up then, explaining her plans for a winter garden. "Though if this weather continues, Hugh, I do not know how well it will do."

Bear, treading gently, waited for her to suggest they retire for the night, but took the initiative when she yawned for the third time. "You are tired, Rosa."

"I am," she sounded surprised. "You do not mind if I…"

Mind? Hardly! "Go on up and get ready, my dear. I will come up in a few minutes."

She blushed. "Oh. Oh yes, of course."

Bear sat sipping his brandy as slowly as he could, watching the hand of the clock creep slowly between the minutes.

Thank goodness she was not a virgin, because his patience had run out and his self-control had become a thread. She had shown interest and even enthusiasm when he kissed her, but had been almost maidenly in her responses. He could understand that, with the servants around and her father likely to call on her at any time. But they would not be disturbed tonight. Jeffreys performed nurse duties, with strict instructions to leave Mr and Mrs Gavenor alone.

Neatham—his father-in-law…a thought to stop him in his tracks —Father Neatham liked Jeffreys, recognized him as a servant from his extreme youth, and accepted his services with equanimity. Even Rosa was not concerned about her father tonight.

She was concerned, though. Edgy and skittish. The aftermath of her hangover? She said she was well, though. Perhaps she was worried about his size? If so, it was further evidence of her relative inexperience. The stories that made her out to be a light woman, to which he had been an unwilling listener and over which he'd punched more than one impudent idiot, were made from whole cloth. The only one he still credited involved old Hurley, the lecherous goat. Hurley had been a little man, by all accounts, with small feet, which was meant to signify a lack of measure in another, more intimate area.

Bear was big as men go, but women were accommodating creatures. He would reassure her and take enough time to make sure she was ready to receive him. All would be well.

At last. Fifteen minutes was enough, surely? He took the stairs two at a time to the room they would share, stripping off his coat, waistcoat, and cravat as he went.

She sat, straight-backed, with her hands folded in her lap and her legs dangling, on the edge of the bed. The night rail she wore obscured her form. It was plain white cotton with a few tucks and pleats and a little white on white embroidery. He would buy her silk and lace to adorn her beauty, teach her to lie waiting for him with the buttons half undone and the soft material draped over her curves.

"Rosa, at last," he said, his mind already removing the night rail to reach the soft flesh beneath. He wriggled out of his shirt, then undid his trousers and let them drop to the floor.

Rosa's eyes fixed on his male parts, proudly upstanding, and her eyes widened.

That thing wasn't going to fit. Rosa had no one she could ask about her marital duties—only guesses and what she'd been unable to avoid observing when she took her goats to the farmer's billy. She knew that men had an appendage similar to the one the billy used. Since her father's injury, she had become used to washing the soft little thing. It was nothing like the object before her, which surely could not have grown under her horrified scrutiny.

"What..." She swallowed and tried again, "What do I need to do?"

He captured both her hands with his and lifted them one at a time to kiss them. "Relax, my wife, and just do what feels good. May I remove your night rail?"

She nodded, and in moments found herself naked, and lying across the middle of the bed, with her new husband beside her, his hands and eyes exploring parts of her no one had seen since she was old enough to bathe herself. And more! *Surely, he doesn't mean to touch me there?*

"Open to me, sweet, and let me..." Whatever else he was thinking went unsaid as he bent in for one of those deep kisses that had been weakening her knees for days.

Her legs widened, almost without her volition, his hand creeping down into the cleft between. The sweet piercing sensation of his touch on her female parts caused an embarrassing gush of the same liquid that had unaccountably leaked when they kissed. Apparently, this was supposed to happen, for he lifted his mouth from hers long enough to murmur approval.

Well then. This was not so bad. This was better than not bad.

She lost herself in sensation, unable to keep from pressing against Bear's lips and his fingers, and his hard, hard body, needing more. Bear moved his lips to her neck, then trailed kisses lower until he could suck her nipple into his mouth, and she arched toward him with a wordless cry of pleasure. He hummed in response, then surged back up to capture her lips again in a hungry kiss, only pulling away to say, "You are ready, are you not, Rosa? I am desperate to be inside you."

Was this the more she wanted? She tensed a little, the eager sensations of seconds ago still there but masked behind apprehension. *But this was what happened in a marriage bed.* "Yes," she said.

He shifted again so he hovered over her, holding his weight on one elbow while the other hand moved between them, adjusting her flesh to fit the blunt knob between them.

Then he thrust, driving all thoughts of pleasure from her mind.

CHAPTER 20

She is too small, Bear realized an instant before she screamed. He had not given her enough time, had not waited for her to adjust. Now it was too late. He was a clumsy, stupid, overgrown fool, and he had hurt his wife.

With a massive effort of will, he ignored the urgent need of his least responsible bodily part and forced himself to still. He lifted himself enough to put a hand either side of her head and look at her face. Tears spilled from her eyes and dripped toward her ears. He wiped them gently with his thumbs.

"Rosa? I'm sorry. I thought you were ready." The last sounded like a whine or an accusation. He hastily added, "I should have taken more care, and more time."

"I am all right, Hugh. I thought… I did not know. I have never done this before."

Bear blinked. In all his ruminations on the probable lovers of the woman he intended to take to wife, he had never considered the possibility there were none. "You were a virgin?" he asked before his brain caught up with his mouth.

Her jaw dropped, and even in the candlelight he could see her turn whiter. "You thought I was not? You believed the stories?

Hugh!" She tried to turn her head to hide the tears, running faster now, but he held her and his body pinned her, and even in the midst of this debacle, his male organ was firmly seated within her and begging him to stop talking and start ravishing.

Which made it hard to think. "No! Not all of them. Just, I thought there must be a seed…some incident long ago. I know you are a virtuous lady, Rosa, and a woman of your word, but girls can be misled by a scoundrel… I've always thought it unfair that Society blames them when so often it is their ignorance and the man's lies to blame." He bent to press a kiss to her lips, but they were as unyielding as stone.

"Rosa." *That was almost a groan.*

"Is it over?" she asked. "Have you finished, Hugh? Because if you have, I would like to wash."

Nothing could be salvaged from tonight except his dignity and hers. "Of course. One moment, please." He withdrew from her as slowly and carefully as he could, an excruciatingly pleasurable torture over all too soon. "I will fetch water. Do you want your night rail?"

They managed a polite and distant exchange of commonplaces as she disappeared behind the screen and managed her ablutions. While she was hidden, he checked the sheet. No blood. Was she making it up, then? No. He would stake his entire fortune on her honesty. Even so, he didn't understand. Didn't virgins bleed?

I *am an idiot,* Rosa thought. Why had she not kept her mouth shut? Bear was too much of a gentleman to point out her shortcomings, but even the dullest and most innocent of ex-maidens could tell that she had failed him. If the formal reserve he donned as soon as got off her was not clue enough, the fact he dressed and left their bedroom, and a short while later the house, would have driven the point home. She watched him hurry through the dark garden to the path that led to Thorne Hall. He would go and wander around the ruins, forgetting his unsatisfactory wife while spinning plans for the refurbishment.

She should have bitten her tongue and kept her scream to herself. The pain—the stretching and burning—had shocked her, but as soon as he stopped moving, the sting began to fade and the fullness was almost pleasant. A little more than almost when he pulled out slowly, so her relief was mixed with regret.

Undoubtedly, he would want to do it again, and next time she would know what to expect. Unless she had given him a distaste for her. On that unpleasant thought, she cried herself to sleep.

Bear returned before dawn, opening the kitchen door with the key he had taken, and shaking his head of the clinging damp before entering the room. The rain must have started again.

"Would you care for a cup of tea?" Rosa asked, and he startled. "I have just boiled the kettle to make one for myself."

"A cup of tea would be welcome." His eyes searched her face, but he didn't speak the question she saw. Was she all right? Was she upset? Was she hurt? He wanted to ask one of those, and she hardly knew the answer to any of them.

She swung the kettle off the fire and ladled the boiling water onto the prepared tea leaves in the pot. "There. We will let it steep for a minute. How long has it been raining?"

"Only ten or fifteen minutes. I was at the ruins. They've made good progress clearing the burnt wing so that it is safe, but this weather will delay our next steps."

Rosa cut a wedge of bread, and another of cheese, then spooned some pickle onto a plate and added a pat of butter. "There," she said, putting it in front of him. "That will keep body and soul together."

"Thank you."

He tucked into the impromptu meal, not meeting her eyes.

Her own questions burned. Would it be like that next time? When would they try again? Had she done something wrong, and if so, what could she do differently? She had only him to ask, and she hardly knew him, though he had seen her naked, had touched her intimately, had prompted reactions from her that made her blush to recall.

When she coloured, he looked alarmed, pushed his empty cup away, and mumbled something about getting into dry clothes, before leaving the kitchen.

He remained courteous but distant all day, spending much of his time with his foreman, and then insisting that Father be brought downstairs to share their meals with them. Rosa responded in kind, hoping they could talk once their bedroom door shut out the world.

Bear spoke first, saying, "You are sore, Rosa. We will not— er," he stopped to consider his words. "We will not exercise our marital rights tonight."

Her relief was matched by her disappointment, and she cast about for a good reason to proceed. "How can I give you a child if we don't..."

"We will be married all our lives. It won't hurt to allow a few days for the soreness to heal." His eyes softened. "I am lucky you did not bar me from our bedroom after that dismal performance last night. If you will forgive me, I promise to amend, once you are no longer wincing when you sit."

That was all. He stripped to his shirt, but no further, climbed into his side of the bed, turned his back, and fell asleep within minutes.

The next two days—and nights—were the same. Cautious courtesy, little real conversation, and no more caressing touches or passionate kisses. Rosa had often wished for a woman in whom she could really confide, but never more than now. If only she could put her head in her mother's lap and pour out her confusion and her questions. She had long, imaginary conversations with Aunt Lillibelle, who had lived a wicked life according to the entire village, so was just the person to advise Rosa now. The questions were clear enough, but the imaginary Aunt Lillibelle only knew what Rosa knew, so her questions went unanswered.

Then, four mornings after their wedding, a courier arrived with Bear's weekly package of letters from Liverpool, and everything changed again.

CHAPTER 21

"I won't be above a month," Bear told his wife, "but if this opportunity is everything Lion says, we stand to make a fortune, Rosa. You have everything you need?"

"Yes, yes. You have given me money enough for a full quarter, and we shall be perfectly comfortable, Hugh. You do not need to worry about us."

"Caleb has everything well in hand at the Hall, but if he comes up against a problem and needs a decision, I have told him to ask you. We've discussed enough about my plans, I'm confident you will know what must be done."

"You trust me with your business?"

"You are my wife. It is our business. You won't have to concern yourself with the other properties and investments. The couriers will come after me. But you are right on hand at Thorne Hall. You are a clever woman with good instincts. I would be a fool not to trust you. You will write to let me know if you need me, or anything I can give you?"

He did not want to go; not with things unresolved. However, his wife held him at arm's-length with a cool reserve that spoke of the depth of her hurt at his wrongful assumption. Not that she stopped caring for his ordinary needs. Rosa, he was coming to understand, couldn't stop nurturing if she tried. She sent food to the Hall when he did not come for meals, had hot baths ready for him when he returned home, stood arm-in-arm with him to present a united front when some of the more prosperous villagers called to congratulate them. Which did not, he noted, include the Pelmans or the Thrextons.

She did it all with a dignified reserve, as the gap between them widened day by day. He didn't dare touch her, for the taste of her was blazoned on his soul and he would not be able to stop at a touch. No more caresses. No more kisses. Not until she was ready to be his wife in truth, because where she was concerned, he did not trust himself to keep his appetites in check.

This trip might be a godsend, taking him away from the constant temptation she represented and giving her time to forget his clumsiness and stupidity.

"The horses are ready, sir," Jeffreys said.

"I'll be there in a minute," Bear replied. Now. This was the one exception. With Jeffreys waiting by the horses, he would not have time to let the brute in his trousers off its leash, so giving his wife one last kiss was as safe as he could make it.

Rosa was agreeing. What to? Oh yes, she would write. "And you must write too, Hugh. Travel is uncertain at the best of times, and this weather makes it chancier. Please write every few days just so that I know you are well."

She would worry about him. He couldn't stop his lips curving at the thought, fool man. Undoubtedly, being Rosa, she would worry about Jeffreys, too, and the horses. "Of course, I will." He hesitated. Before their wedding, he had hauled her into several very pleasant kisses, but he was nervous about initiating this one. "May I kiss you goodbye, dear wife?"

Her eyes widened, and she smiled before stepping closer with her face up. "Farewell, please. I do want you to come home, Hugh."

Better than he expected and much more than he deserved. Rather like the kiss itself, which left him adjusting with some difficulty to the saddle as they rode down through the village and out to the coast and the ferry.

*I've sent this letter with Makepeace Brownlee, who comes highly recommended as a nurse for elderly gentlemen who are a bit confused in their minds. If you and your father like him, I thought he could relieve the servants of the night-care duties, but you must organize the household as you wish.*

I have a brief stopover in Manchester to meet with a potential buyer for the townhouse I told you about there, then straight to London to meet with the Earl of Ruthford. The weather continues uncertain, but…

The rest of the letter contained commonplaces that could have been written to anyone, except that it began 'My dear wife' and ended 'Your husband, Hugh Gavenor.'

She looked at those words for a long time, more than half tempted to kiss them, but Brownlee was waiting, regarding her with calm brown eyes. He was a man in his middle years, sturdily built, with pleasant features and a face that fell naturally into laugh lines. Instinctively, she felt she could trust him with her father, but she asked him questions about his previous positions, and then took him upstairs to meet Father.

Father sulked in his chair by the fire, and rounded on Rosa as soon as she entered. "Rosie, I don't know what you are about, keeping such a maid. She refuses to bring me my trousers and my boots, and I must away to Thorne Hall. I am already very late, and what will Lord Hurley be thinking?"

Sukie, the calmer and kinder of the sisters Bear had hired, had her lips tightly pressed together and one cheek bore the imprint of a palm in fading scarlet.

"Oh Father," Rosa said. "Oh Sukie, I am so sorry."

"Didn't move quite fast enough, Mrs Gavenor. Don't you worry none. But how to calm him, I do not know."

Brownlee addressed Father directly. "Dressing you will be my job now, sir. I am Brownlee, and I have been hired to look after you."

"A valet? Lord Hurley has hired me a valet? How very kind of him." Father frowned. "I had one. He has gone off somewhere. Do you mean to stay, Brown? Eh?"

"For as long as you need me, sir," Brownlee replied, unperturbed by the truncating of his name. "If you give me a minute to find out where things are, I will have your clothes directly."

Rosa's face must have expressed her alarm, because Brownlee murmured, "A short walk will do him no harm, and will help to turn his mind elsewhere, ma'am, if you permit."

"He does not like to be carried," Rosa warned.

"Just downstairs. Mr Gavenor's purchases for Mr Neatham's comfort should be offloaded by now, and we shall put the invalid's chair to use immediately. Now, Miss— Sukie was it? Would you be kind enough to show me how Mr Neatham likes his things to be kept?"

Father beamed. "I like this one better than the big fellow, Rosie."

Rosa, as she later examined the other items her big fellow had sent for her father's comfort, disagreed with her father. She liked the big fellow a lot. Far more than was comfortable, given the constrained atmosphere between them.

Still, the parting kiss had been promising. Plus, he had thought of her in Liverpool; had sent her all these things and Brownlee to ease her load. She pulled his letter from her pinafore pocket and, looking around quickly to make sure she was unobserved, pressed a kiss to his signature.

CHAPTER 22

Bear detoured to spend a few days in Birmingham, where a run-down block of townhouses built early in the last century was being sold to fund the owner's interest in racehorses. Back at his hotel, after spending the day going over the derelicts with a local builder, he found his mail had caught up with him, which included a letter from his wife.

Had she liked his present? He had realized afterwards that he'd bought her nothing personal, and had shopped that afternoon to remedy the lack. A package containing a length of figured green and gold silk for a gown, a pretty bonnet, and a shawl in the same tones sat waiting for him to pen a note to go with them. Should he have purchased jewellery, as well? He hadn't been able to interpret her reaction to the ring, and as things stood, didn't want to risk giving her an item she might see as suitable for a mistress.

Especially since he wouldn't be there to see her face when she opened the package.

But a man might buy his wife a gown and bonnet, surely?

He put the letter to one side and dealt with the business correspondence first, but his eyes kept drifting to Rosa's letter. Did she miss him? He snorted at the thought. After four days of marriage, and most of them awkward? She missed him like a sore tooth, no doubt.

The letter, when he could put it off no longer, was oddly reassuring. She thanked him for Brownlee and the few things he'd sent to make the care of the invalid more convenient. He'd done nothing that required thanks. She was his wife, and his duty was to provide for her care, which meant caring for her father.

She reported on the wellbeing of the household, with a couple of anecdotes that brought a smile. She had resolved a small dispute on the building site by instructing them to move the planned ice pit to the shaded side of the house, and the kitchen door so that it opened onto that part of the courtyard. She hoped she had not overstepped her authority. He checked the sketches and nodded. She was quite correct.

She addressed the letter to 'Honoured Sir,' but the signature was a little more encouraging. 'Yours truly, Rosa.' She said nothing about the village. Perhaps the weather had been too poor for her to make the trip. He hoped she was having no further trouble with the squire's mother and the Pelmans. The marriage should have spiked their guns, but Bear still could not be easy.

For the dozenth time since he'd ridden away, he wanted to turn back, sort out his marriage, and not leave again until he could bring her away with him. As if they loved one another. As if they wanted to live in one another's pockets. No. He had work to do, and so did she. If she met with a problem she couldn't manage, she would tell him. Would't she?

The villagers had divided into two camps. In some ways, Rosa had been more comfortable when she'd been the outsider—the leper who lived in the desert, was avoided by everyone, and stayed out of their way as best she could.

Marriage changed everything. Not for the Pelmans and the Thrextons, who would not acknowledge her existence, but continued to talk about her behind her back, and sometimes right in front of her—though without naming names. They had their supporters, too; people who were happy to believe the worst of her, especially if it curried favour with the gentry.

On the other hand, more people than she expected were prepared to take up the cause of the new Mrs Gavenor, whose husband employed half the village and paid liberally. No. That was a little unfair. Several people had explained, shamefaced, that they had never believed the scurrilous lies, but had felt unable to stand up against the most prominent members of the village. Now that Bear stood behind her, and had turned the Rector to her support, they were pleased to welcome her back into their lives, their shops, and their parlours.

Being a bone of contention in the village meant trying not to aggravate one side while soothing the other, especially when her champions resorted to fisticuffs, as happened in her husband's work crew not long after she received his first letter.

Rosa arrived for the aftermath, the foreman Caleb Redding wading into a free-for-all and laying about liberally to separate those who refused to stop throwing punches.

"There's the whore now," one of the men muttered when he noticed her, prompting another scuffle and a roar from Caleb, "The next man to throw a punch or make a foul remark is dismissed!"

Should she leave? To do so felt like running away, and she was tired of hiding, but now all the men watched her. She felt the weight of their scorn, lust and derision, but also respect, admiration and even some sort of heroine worship, which sat as heavily on her as the more negative distortions of her true self.

Caleb spoke before she could decide what to do. "Mrs Gavenor, I apologize for the men. No lady should have to see such brutality. We had a meeting, did we not? Can I ask you to wait at the tent for a few minutes while I have a further word to the men? I will join you shortly."

Rosa took two steps away before she stopped. 'It is our business', Bear had said. The men worked for Bear and therefore they worked for her. "If you have no objection, Mr Redding, I will stay. My husband has authorized me to act as his representative here, as you know. I have full confidence in your ability to handle trouble in the work team, but it is my responsibility to see that justice and peace both prevail. Also, from what I heard as I approached"—she looked around the group, noting who glared back and who would not meet her eyes—"the matter of the fight concerns me closely. I am also owed some justice, I think."

Caleb examined her face, then nodded. "Very well. Hiram, fetch a chair for Mrs Gavenor."

One of the younger men ran to the tent that Caleb used as his onsite office and came back with a folding chair he set up next to Caleb, the men in a wide ring around him—two groups, mutually glaring.

The 'pro-Gavenors' outnumbered the others, Rosa noted, which should have eased her, but still her heart pounded and her mouth dried. "I have something to say, Mr Redding," she said, as firmly as she could. Here, on her own property, with her own workers, she had to take a stand, or forever be a victim of Pelman and Lady Threxton.

She met Caleb's anxious eyes and must have appeared more confident than she felt, because he nodded encouragement.

"From what I heard, those who were fighting have taken sides in the village scandal, arguing over whether I am the innocent victim of lies or the lightskirt that my persecutors paint me. Trial by combat is rather old fashioned, gentlemen. However, here you have the person who knows what has happened and what has not happened. I will answer questions, but first I want you to know this."

She composed her skirts around her as she thought carefully about her words.

"My husband and I are providing work in this village. Work for all of you. You will have heard, and it is true, that we intend to bring Thorne Hall back to its former glory and sell it to a family who will need servants and who will buy local services."

She paused to allow them time to grumble agreement.

"I welcome the opportunity to defend myself from the accusations against me, especially since—for two years—my accusers have spoken behind my back so I could not hear the charges nor refute them. It is only fair to tell you that I fully support Mr Redding. While I cannot and do not wish to tell you what to think, nor can I control what you say off this work site, you will not insult my husband and his honour by showing disrespect of any kind to me while taking his coin." She swung her head to look at her supporters. "Nor will Mr Redding or I tolerate fighting on this site, whether it is for or against me. Am I clear?"

Another round of nods and grumbles.

"Very well. Who wishes to ask the first question?"

Put on the spot, they were reluctant to start, but at last one burly fellow—a local villager rather than one of Gavenor's Liverpool imports—said, "They say as the squire's your cousin, and he don't like you much, ma'am. That's a fact, is it?"

The token honorific helped Rosa to answer calmly with a little family history, and her own surprise at the discovery. "Families can be difficult," she added, and her sigh was echoed by others.

"You should meet my mother-in-law," one man said. "Twenty years married to her daughter, and she still hates me because she wanted a better marriage for the lass. Well, I love my wife. That has to count for something, doesn't it?"

Nods, then, and an undefinable sense of relaxation, until the next man asked, "Is it true you lived here in Thorne Hall with the old baron?"

"I lived here with my father, who was the baron's librarian, until my father could no longer perform his duties. After that, my father and I moved to Rose Cottage, though the baron continued to live at the Hall until he died at the time of the fire. And, gentlemen, I have heard the rumours that the baron took me as mistress. Not when those rumours first appeared, which was two years ago, and four years after the baron's death; eight years after I moved from Thorne Hall. If they were true, would servants not have talked at the time?" She raised her brows, fixing the man who had asked the question with her gaze.

"Think about that. I would also ask you to consider that the baron was a man in his sixties and I was a much younger woman than I am now, and under the care and protection of my father."

"She's right," said one of the local men. "Me ma worked at the Hall when Mrs Gavenor was living there, and she always says there isn't nothing to them stories."

"Servants always know," Rosa agreed.

Afterward, the tone warmed, and when Caleb sent the men back to their work, he congratulated her. "You won't have won them all over, Mrs Gavenor," he warned, "but you've gone a long way with the fair ones. And the others'll keep their mouths shut if they value their jobs."

From that day, she saw a slow increase in the number of people who nodded politely when she passed, or who spoke to her in the churchyard as she left Sunday services. She even had afternoon callers now, and servants enough that she could sit and dispense tea and hold a conversation. She made afternoon calls, watching the lady of the house closely to refresh her mother's half-remembered lessons in hostess etiquette, given over tea parties with an assortment of dolls. One of Bear's reasons for marrying was to have a hostess, so she practiced assiduously.

Perhaps, when he returned, they could have guests to dinner, though with the Pelmans and Thrextons still her enemies, it was a puzzle to know how to fill a table.

The unseasonable rain and cold continued, threatening the harvest, and Father caught an ague from one of the maids, which meant Rosa's trips to the village were curtailed since she did not like to leave him. The ague was taking its toll of the village, Mrs Gilly-wether told her. Even the rector was confined to bed, unable to perform any of his duties.

The maid recovered quickly and was soon back at work, but Father's ague went to his chest. The doctor from the next village, who examined him, looked grave as he prescribed mustard plasters and a strong-smelling mixture for Father to breathe. The odorous mixture set Father coughing and sneezing so violently, Rosa and Brownlee feared he would simply stop breathing.

In the worry of Father's illness, Bear's frivolous present from

Birmingham was a welcome distraction. Rosa held up the silk before her in front of the mirror. Her reflection was pale with worry and heavy eyed. "You do not do credit to this lovely fabric," she informed herself, but she smiled anyway. *A new silk frock!* Who would have thought, just two months ago, that an expedition to pick roses would bring her a husband who could afford to clothe her in silk?

She modelled the bonnet and the shawl for the edification of her mirror-image. What exquisite taste Bear had. "He wants you to reflect credit on him," she scolded, shaking her finger at Rosa-in-the-mirror. "Do not think this gift means more than that."

She read again the pertinent part of his letter.

> *"I have every intention of seeing you dressed as befits my wife, but until we can get to London, or at least to Liverpool, I hope you can find someone local to make this fabric into a gown for Sunday services and for visiting. I will send more as I can. My wife should look as prosperous as any in the district."*

In other words, this was more of an investment than a gift, and she would be wise to remember that.

However, she could not resist a final peek in the mirror, where the bonnet framed her face, making her look almost pretty, and the glowing colours of the shawl fitted softly around her curves.

CHAPTER 23

In London, Bear had a standing invitation to stay with the Earl and Countess of Ruthford in their townhouse on Hanover Square. His lordship was in residence, the butler informed him, but her ladyship remained in the country. Since Lion and Dorothea were unfashionably attached to one another, Bear felt a certain alarm. Lion would undoubtedly explain when he returned from whatever errand had taken him out.

He and Jeffreys were shown to their usual room, and Jeffreys went off to fetch water while Bear stared out the window, thinking about his own wife. He had received a charming letter thanking him for the silk and other gifts, with a sketch of the gown she was having made. Two more letters had arrived since, in response to further packages. Buying gifts to send to his wife was rapidly becoming a habit, but he would rather have her with him.

He looked around the bedroom—a comfortable, if anonymous, space that had suited him well for years. A single man didn't need a townhouse in London. He could stay with friends or at his club, or take rooms with a landlady who cooked, or board in a rooming house and buy his food at nearby cookhouses.

A married man needed a house his wife could turn into a home.

Perhaps, while he was in London, he should look for a place he could rent—or perhaps buy. After all, a sound property in London was always a good investment.

Jeffreys returned with hot water and the news that Lord Ruthford had returned and awaited Mr Gavenor in his study, "Once you have time to freshen yourself, sir."

Bear washed and changed, then hurried downstairs. He didn't bother with ceremony, but let himself into the study and stood for a moment watching his friend at work. Lion looked well. Their leader was a couple of years younger than Bear, with searching brown eyes, usually alight with humour. They became a devastating weapon when they turned cold. Lion had inherited his thick dark hair from a grandmother, who had been a local girl his mother's father had married while stationed in India.

"Are you coming in?" Lion asked and looked up, one corner of his mouth lifting in half a grin. "Good Lord! You don't get any smaller, do you? One forgets, and then there you are, taking up half the room. Help yourself to coffee, man, and be sure to pick a sturdy chair."

Lion was nearly as tall as Bear, but a thoroughbred to Bear's carthorse. "Sturdy? All of your chairs are made of matchsticks. If they collapse under me, I hope you'll ship my poor remains home to my wife."

Lion's eyebrows shot toward his hairline. "Wife? Since when do you have a wife?"

Bear had not intended to announce his change in matrimonial status quite so bluntly, but he was not displeased with the effect. He poured a cup of thick black coffee, drawing out the moment. Lion served it Turkish fashion, but the tray contained hot water and cream for guests who preferred a blander version.

Bear diluted his coffee and turned from the tray to find his former officer sitting straight behind his desk, hands folded on his blotter, eyes steady on Bear's face. A faint smile playing around his mouth. "Confession time, my son. Tell Father Lion everything. Whom have you married, when, and why?"

Bear said nothing while he brought his coffee to the desk and seated himself on one of the robust chairs that Lion's wife had bought for her husband's sanctuary. "For you are mostly giants," she had informed his friends, "and I want you all to be comfortable."

Lion raised an eyebrow at Bear's continued silence. "That bad?"

"Not bad. Just…complicated." Where to begin?

"Surely, not one of the London debutantes you were so scathing about this past Season, poor little girls."

"Poor little feather-wits and rapacious harpies."

"So you said in April, to my wife's despair, for she had introduced you to the nicest girls she knew."

"Not her fault. I was too old for them, Lion, as you observed at the time."

"And too nice for a widow. Have you married a widow?"

"I wasn't against marrying a widow. Just not one who was having such a good time kicking up her heels in London that I feared spending my remaining days waiting for her to bump me off so she could do it again, with my money."

"Avoiding the question, Bear? How bad is it? Sorry. Complicated."

"She's not too young. Not too old, either. Thirty-six."

Lion said nothing, but his eyebrows lifted.

How to explain Rosa. Bear was barely conscious of the helpless wave of his hand as he considered and rejected several sentences. "She suits me, Lion."

"A pertinent fact, but not a history. I can see an interrogation is required. What is the name of this not-old lady, and where did you meet?"

"Rosa. Rosabel Neatham. I found her on a ladder picking my roses." Once he started, the story came easily. "Then a few days after the wedding, I got your message and came to London. So I hope you're in a hurry to get back to Lady Ruthford, for I do not mean to linger here one day more than I need to."

"I beg your pardon? A few days after the wedding? You married this paragon then abandoned her a few days after the wedding? Why on earth didn't you write back and tell me to go soak my head?"

Bear's guilty wince didn't go unnoticed.

"You and the lady have had a falling out."

"Not precisely. Rosa doesn't… That is to say, I thought some distance might help, but Rosa is not one to nurse a grudge. She writes charming letters, and I write back. When I get home, we will put it behind us."

"If you will take advice from a man married four years longer than you, when you get back to Mrs Gavenor, discuss whatever it was and clear up any misunderstandings. She is very likely blaming herself for whatever came between you. Women do."

"Surely not! It was my fault entirely. At least… Lion, I thought virgins bled." *Lord. I did not say that out loud, did I?*

Lion took a sip of coffee. "Not that my experience is vast, but I don't believe it to be an inevitable rule. It depends on the age of the woman, on what kinds of physical activities she has done—my own wife… Well. Let's leave it at that. And the man's patience is important."

Bear groaned. "I should probably be hanged."

"I see."

He probably did, too. The ability to pick up small clues and draw correct conclusions was one of his great assets as a commander, and he knew Bear better than anyone else in the world.

"You believed the rumours about her and you still married her?"

"No! At least, I thought they were mostly malicious lies. They started only after her father was no longer able to protect her, and the people most assiduous in pushing them all had an axe to grind."

"This Pelman wanted to coerce her into bed and used the family feud with her respectable cousins."

"In a nutshell. Dammit, Lion, it's obvious to me now. She kissed like an innocent. I thought she was just shy, or nervous about being interrupted by the servants."

"Ah well. Women are told their first time will be painful, though it is not necessarily so." He smiled as if at a fond memory, then recalled himself and continued. "You made sure she enjoyed her second time, I assume." He raised his brows again. "No. You rushed off to London, instead. Bear, tell me you didn't let the poor lady know you thought she had had previous lovers."

Bear grimaced.

"You did." Lion wagged his head from side to side. "Bear, Bear, what are we going to do with you? So, there she is miserable in Cheshire because her husband insulted then abandoned her. Here you are miserable in London because you have made a mess of things and don't know how to put it right. Go home, Bear. Talk to your wife."

CHAPTER 24

Two weeks of mostly fine weather saw the standing part of
Thorne Hall made weather tight, and had the local farmers
scurrying to salvage what they could of the harvest. Papa seemed
slightly better, too, enjoying daily outings in his chair as he lectured
Brownlee on herbal lore and the romance poetry of medieval
France.

Rosa's new gown was delivered, and she wore it with the new
bonnet and shawl to Matins on the second fine Sunday, feeling
guilty delight at outshining Livia Pelman and the younger Lady
Threxton. With an effort, she reminded herself that she was here to
pray, not to show off her fine feathers, and she did penance by
praying for the two women.

They lingered outside, talking to the vicar who had ridden over
from a neighbouring parish since the rector had gone to stay with
relatives for his convalescence. The vicar was a young man, new to
the area, and employed to cover the parish for a rector who had a
second parish, and one he preferred, in Lancashire.

"The wages of sin, I assure you," Rosa heard Miss Pelman say
to him.

Rosa set her jaw, straightened her back and swept up to them, holding out her hand to the vicar as the other two drew away as if to avoid contamination. "Vicar Snaith. I am Mrs Hugh Gavenor. My husband and I own and are restoring Thorne Hall. I see you have already met my cousin, Lady Threxton, and her friend.

The vicar, with a nervous glance at the two women, tentatively took her hand and bowed slightly. "Mrs Gavenor. Ah… Er…"

Before he could figure out a way to avoid taking sides, or decide which side to take, a relief force of Rosa's supporters joined them, introducing themselves and taking over the conversation. Miss Pelman and Lady Threxton withdrew, and the vicar, though not without several sideways glances at Rosa, accepted her presence in the middle of the chattering group.

"She hasn't improved none," Mrs Gillywether said as they made their way home. "That Livia Pelman was a mean child and she has grown into a mean old woman."

Rosa turned to look at her. "You knew Miss Pelman as a child? But I thought they only came here six years ago."

"Came back six years ago," Mrs Gillywether corrected. "That Mr Pelman who caused all the trouble for the squire's girls? He brought his two little 'uns to live at Thorne Hall when he came to be factor for Lord Hurley. Miss Livia was six and Master Lawrence just old enough to toddle. Before your time, that was, Mrs Gavenor. Lord Hurley dismissed him after he ruined poor Miss Belle."

By the middle of the following week, the storms had returned. Caleb was feeling smug, since he had moved himself and the Liverpool crew out of the tents in the stables and into Thorne Hall, where they continued to camp, but without risk of a cold drenching in the middle of the night.

"Now the place is weather tight, we can continue the work no matter how it storms, Mrs Gavenor. And we've done the demolition needed to make the place safe. We'll carry on with that and the new stable block in fine spells, and make the inside what it needs to be when it rains."

Rosa walked through the rain to inspect progress and was given an attic-to-cellars guided tour. The camp cook had set up in the old-fashioned kitchen, where the fireplaces and even the bread oven continued to function, though little else remained of the fittings. Better than the tent kitchen he had been using, but still… Rosa returned home thinking furiously, and sent for Caleb the following afternoon.

"Mr Redding, I propose a change to Mr Gavenor's work schedule. He intends Thorne Hall to have a fully modern kitchen with one of the new closed stoves. If you order that immediately and put it in when it arrives, your cook will be able to do a far more efficient job of feeding the workers. In fact, I propose you finish the kitchen according to Mr Gavenor's plan, and the servant hall alongside, and make full use of it while you complete the hall. Well fed, comfortable men will work more efficiently, I believe."

Caleb approved once they'd talked through the suggestion, but his parting comment gave Rosa pause. "If Mr Gavenor is not happy, I shall tell him that he left his authority with you, ma'am."

After he left, Rosa went to her desk to fetch Bear's letter that had arrived the day before and reread it. She had written to him about every decision she had made on the site, and every response she received endorsed her thinking. On the other hand, Caleb reported back to Bear, as well. Was Bear saying something different in his letters to Caleb? Would he be unhappy with her change to the timeline, to finish the kitchen first? Surely, he would see the sense of it.

"I will be in London tomorrow, and I hope on my way back to you not long after," he had written. 'To you,' not to Thorne Hall or Kettlesworth. The thrill at the undoubtedly accidental choice of words had to be suppressed before she continued.

> *"I will look forward to seeing you in all your finery and will add to the store when I arrive. I'm also excited about seeing progress on Thorne Hall. Caleb writes that your plan to keep the nearest, undamaged part of the destroyed wing has given us an extra room on each floor and provides visual balance to the exterior. Well done."*

There. See? She was an asset to the business and should not read more into his comments than that. Still, being appreciated for any reason was a rare enough experience. To ask for more would be greedy.

He would return to Rose Cottage and she would be here to welcome him, showing no resentment and making no demands. That was the way forward, was it not? She had let him see her pain, both physical and emotional, on the night of her wedding, and he had withdrawn and then fled. If only she had someone to advise her on how to repair the damage and lure him back to her bed.

He would come, would he not? From what she had observed, men were creatures of appetite, and besides, Bear had been blunt about his desire for an heir. If his words or his body parts hurt her again, she would find a way to conceal her pain.

The door knocker sounded. Who could have come visiting in this weather? Rosa folded Bear's letter and placed it with the others in her desk.

Maggie, whose turn it was to answer the door today, vibrated with excitement, her eyes round, and a huge grin on her face. "Ma'am, there is a Mrs Belle Clifford wishes to know if she might come in."

"Belle Clifford?" *Mother's sister? The wicked aunt?* "Yes. Yes, of course."

Rosa stood and smoothed her hands down her skirts. Thank goodness she had chosen one of her new gowns this morning. She had never dreamt that her aunt would reply to her letter in person. What would Bear think?

The woman who entered before Rosa could fret herself into flinders was no bigger than Rosa herself. She leant heavily on the arm of a footman. Rosa took one look at the white face, an older version of her own, and darted forward. "Oh, but you are not well. Here, bring her to the couch. Let us make you comfortable."

"Thank you," her aunt said, her low voice melodious. "I do not travel well. You are very kind."

Rosa and the footman lowered the frail woman onto a sofa, and Rosa plumped cushions for her to rest against, then fetched a knitted rug to cover her legs.

"Maggie, see that Mrs Clifford's servants are made comfortable." *How many servants? And where would they all sleep?* Rosa would think of something. "Ask cook to send up tea and light refreshments. Or coffee, Mrs Clifford?"

"Tea would be delightful. I thank you."

Maggie and the footman exited the room, leaving Rosa and her wicked aunt alone. The lady didn't look wicked. She wore no paint on her face to hide her wrinkles. She had removed her hat and outer coat, and her hair, confined in a neat roll at the back of her head, was streaked with grey. The jacket and skirt she wore were fashionable, but not revealing.

She endured Rosa's examination without comment, but her voice was amused when she said, "You know who I am."

Rosa nodded. "You are my mother's sister. My Aunt Lillibelle." *Or perhaps my mother. Dare I ask?*

"I was not sure you would agree to see me," Aunt Lillibelle said.

"I wrote."

"So did Rosie, but Albert never consented to a visit."

Rosie shook her head, more in disbelief than denial. "My mother wrote to you? But… I was told you had died."

"So you said in your letter. Not yet, as you can see. Though I have a cancer, the doctors say, and will not long survive my Raithby." Aunt Lillibelle caressed the locket pinned to her lapel, a smile curving her lips.

"Lord Raithby is dead?"

"These four weeks, but dear Glimmerston gave me your letter. Or Raithby, I suppose I must learn to say. My Raithby's eldest, and such a nice boy. So, when I needed somewhere to go, I thought of Kettlesworth, and I suddenly longed to see you. And here I am."

"I am glad," Rosa said, firmly squashing errant thoughts about the likely reactions of Bear and the villagers.

"Is your father out?" Aunt Lillibelle asked. "I quite expected him to refuse me the door."

"My father is…" How to explain her father? Before she could begin, Maggie and Sukie carried in trays with cups and milk and sugar, and some of cook's little cakes. Aunt Lillibelle's footman followed with the urn and the teapot on a tray, and the locked tea cabinet that had been one of Bear's presents.

She directed the servants to put the makings down within her reach and dismissed them again. Aunt Lillibelle stayed silent until they left, leaning back on her pillows, her eyes shut.

"Rosie used to write to me about you, her little Rosa. She said you looked like me, and she was right. I suppose that cannot have been easy in this village. I am sorry if my foolish choices have caused you to suffer."

"Lady Threxton never forgave you. Or me either."

"Amanda Threxton? What hurt did she take? Her father jettisoned poor Rosie quickly enough, which was so unjust, for she had nothing to do with my running away! Thank goodness for Albert. You must not think I blame him for keeping me away. He did what he needed to protect my sister, and later you. I would not have come now, Mrs Gavenor, except you wrote to me. Also, I needed to leave Trenton and I wanted to see my home one more time."

"Milk? Sugar? And please call me Rosa. You are my aunt, after all."

"Just black, Rosa. Thank you. Would it be too much to call me Aunt Belle? Just while I am here?"

"Aunt Belle, then. But you cannot be planning to travel on in this weather."

"I have no wish to…" Whatever Aunt Belle planned to say was interrupted as she bent double with a spasm of coughing.

Rosa jumped up to see if she could help, patting her aunt gently on the back. "But you are not well. You will stay here tonight. I will have a room made up."

When Aunt Belle could speak again, she protested, "But your father… And the maid called you Mrs Gavenor. Your husband will not approve of your scandalous aunt, Rosa."

Rosa refused to consider either of the men who had, in their different ways, left her to make her own decisions. "Father lives in dreams of the past, and my husband is away. Even if he were here, I am sure he would be the first to say I cannot send any sick woman out into weather like this, let alone my own mother's sister. No. You must stay. At least until the weather is fine and you can continue your journey. Where are you going, Aunt Belle?"

Aunt Belle shrugged, dabbing at her mouth with a handkerchief that now bore flecks of blood, before she answered, "Here to the Wirral. I thought to find a small cottage, perhaps down by the shore. I do not have long to live, Rosa. I have been forbidden to die in my own home. I thought perhaps I could die in the homeland of my childhood."

Father was well enough for dinner but became distressed when introduced to his sister-in-law. "Have I met you before?" he asked. "I knew a Belle once, but she went to London and died. She was much younger than you. A mere child, really. You missed her, didn't you, Rosie? A foolish child, and spoilt, but you loved her."

"She was a loving woman, your mother," Belle murmured to Rosa, when Brownlee distracted Father by directing his attention to a dish of spiced mushrooms.

After dinner, Brownlee helped Father up to his bed chamber, and Rosa ordered tea served in the parlour. "Or would you prefer to go straight to bed yourself, Aunt Belle?"

"A cup of tea, and then bed. I grow tired easily, and Maud fusses."

Maud was the maid Aunt Belle had brought with her, and a more unlikely maid for a courtesan, Rosa could not imagine. Maud was a good decade older than her mistress, buttoned to the neck and the cuff in dark, serviceable cotton with crisp white cuffs and collar, her gray hair tightly confined under a cap. She would not have seemed at all out of place as maid to the Rector's wife, if the rector had a wife.

Aunt Belle did not much resemble Rosa's imaginings, either. She had sent her coachman, two footmen, and another maid on to the inn, keeping only Maud beside her; five servants, a luxurious carriage, and a mountain of baggage. Her clothing was of the highest quality, as Rosa might have expected. The wages of sin, as Livia Penman would call them, were clearly high.

On the other hand, the garments were cut like those any older lady of the parish might wear, if she had good taste and a deep purse. And Aunt Belle did not wear paint, or if she did, it was not obvious, and her manners and language were as refined as Rosa's own.

The eyes so like her own were examining Rosa as she brought Aunt Belle her tea.

"You are full of questions, Rosa. I shall answer anything I can." She took a cautious sip of the hot liquid as Rosa returned to fetch her own tea, a dozen questions fighting for first place on her tongue.

The one that escaped was, "Will you teach me how to attract a man?"

Aunt Belle raised her eyebrows. "Now, that is not the question I expected. Your husband?"

"Yes. Hugh."

"Bear Gavenor. I have read about him in the London papers. My dear, you shall tell me all about him and I will help you however I can."

Aunt Belle had dark bruises under her eyes, and the hands holding the tea cup trembled. "Tomorrow," Rosa suggested. "You are tired, and I must not keep you from your bed."

"Poor Rosa, with two invalids on your hands. You look like me, my dear, but you have your mother's kind heart. It is a wonderful gift, but can be a terrible burden if you take no care of your own needs. Have an early night yourself, and we shall talk tomorrow."

CHAPTER 25

It wasn't as simple as walking out that afternoon and heading for
Cheshire. Even Lion agreed they should take a look at the
terraces that the Earl of Denthorpe was selling, to see whether they
could be made over into housing for the upwardly-mobile
merchants that wanted what Bear had to sell. Denthorpe held title
to estates in three locations, and Bear and Lion each had their own
reasons for seeing all three as soon as they could. The earl's agent
agreed to meet them at the first property the following morning,
then conduct them to each of the others.

Bear knew as soon as they arrived at the first address that it
would not do. "Not for me, Lion. In this area? Not my market."

"We're here," Lion argued. "We might as well take a look."

"If you've an interest in rentals for skilled craftsmen and the like.
But wealthy merchants who want to live like the gentry? This area is
all wrong for them. They want gardens. They want to get away
from their warehouses and manufactories. They won't buy a townhouse in a terrace in this kind of neighbourhood."

"Really? But the gentry live in townhouses all terraced together.
I do, and I'm a belted, blasted earl."

"Yes, but my merchants don't see it that way. They want a little

"

pocket handkerchief of an estate. A taste of country, with its own detached house or, at most, sharing a wall with another house, but not one on either side. They certainly won't live where they might jostle elbows in the street with their own workers."

"Is there money in housing for skilled craftsmen?" Lion asked.

"Possibly. If the refurbishment isn't too extensive, which you can't altogether calculate till you have the walls off and the ceilings down. Rebuilding can cost more than a whole new build, and only pays if the buyer is willing to pay for the history, or if the builder does things on the cheap. I don't cut corners, Lion, so this one isn't for me."

So, when the agent, Mr Thomas, arrived, they went on to the next location. This was more promising. The earl's father had begun a project ten years ago, copying the successful model of St John's Wood. "His lordship ran into difficulties when the builder absconded with the architect's wife, funding the escape—as they later discovered—by substituting inferior materials for the second story brick work. With poor harvests and the war, the extra invest- ment needed to finish the project was just not available, so the houses, some of them near finished, have been sitting abandoned ever since. "

It was a small development, just ten groups of two houses, each set on a large plot of land—currently a wilderness of scrub, weeds, and building materials. The gardens would need to be landscaped, and fenced to give privacy. The earl's troubles had meant four of the buildings—eight houses—were not weather-tight. Some attempts had been made to protect them, but not recently. In consequence, vagrants, animals, and invasive plants had encroached upon the buildings that were least secure.

The three men rambled all over the area, then adjourned to a nearby public house for a tankard of ale and a pie.

"His lordship's price?" Bear asked once they had been served.

Thomas named a sum.

Bear snorted.

"For twenty dwellings," Thomas pointed out.

"Twelve, and those needing considerable finishing. The others are only fit to be torn down, which will add cost to the buyer."

They haggled some more, setting the groundwork for later negotiations, since Thomas had the responsibility for making a deal and no authority to do so. Bear hoped the earl would not continue to insist upon making all the decisions while distancing himself from any appearance of interest. Better for everyone if he would directly discuss the estate with Bear or Lion. If he wouldn't, they were all in for a frustrating time.

Bear looked up at the sun to gauge the time. Late afternoon. "Do we have time to look at the third offering?"

"I do not think it will suit you, Mr Gavenor. It is the earl's own townhouse. He spends little time in London and thinks to rent in the future."

"Benford House? Just off Hanover Square?"

At the agent's nod, Bear pursed his lips. "I may have a buyer in mind for that one. Shall we go?"

Once they returned to Lion's phaeton, with Thomas following behind in his chaise, Lion objected. "I thought you said merchants were not interested in terraced houses. Besides, the neighbours on the square will not be amused if you plant a mushroom in their midst."

Bear shot him an amused grin. "My buyer is gentry. He dabbles in trade, which is frowned on, but he makes them money, so they tolerate him."

"You, Bear?"

Trust Lion to guess. "I am a married man, after all."

The townhouse was run down, and decorated in a style that suggested that the new Lord Denthorpe's mother had either overseen the refurbishment as a young bride, or had not touched the place during her tenure.

"It will need a lot of work," he said to Lion when they shared a drink in Lion's study later that evening. "But the structure is sound, and I can pay people to redecorate."

"I seem to be making a habit of giving marriage advice," Lion complained, "and it just isn't on, Bear. Once more can't hurt, I suppose. Do the repairs, but let your wife decide on the decoration. It will be her home, after all."

Bear could see the sense of that. "Do you believe that Thomas can get Denthorpe to a meeting?"

"Let's hope so," Lion said, frowning. "I want to go home."

Bear felt the same urge to abandon the deal and hurry north, but the agent seemed certain that Denthorpe was ready to be reasonable. "Next week, he said. But if we could talk directly to Denthorpe, we have a chance of getting everything settled on both properties."

Four more days, and then home to Rosa.

Meanwhile, the shops of London beckoned. Bear found his way to a bookshop, and was searching the shelves for something that might appeal to Rosa when a wife of one of his clients came upon him. "Mr Gavenor, how lovely to see you. Thank you so much for the estate you sold us. We are loving it."

They chatted for a few minutes, and Bear disclosed his errand. Shortly afterwards, he posted a book of poetry that the client's wife had recommended, and a short note. He hoped Rosa would enjoy both.

The next day, Lion agreed to join a present-hunting expedition, buying two dolls, some board books, a box of wooden blocks painted in bright colours, and a large rocking horse for his daughter, who was not quite two. When Bear suggested the horse might be a little premature, Lion insisted, "She will grow into it."

Bear found a silver set for a lady's dressing table that included a brush, mirror, comb, several trinket boxes, and a tray. They were all inlaid with ivory on which some talented artist had painted a fantasy scene of flowers, with fairies dressed in petals and wearing caps and bonnets formed from bell-like blooms.

"This for Rosa," he announced, and pursed his lips when he realized Lion had noticed him smiling at the picture on the back of the mirror. His smile crept back as soon as he turned his back on Lion. Fairies for his fairy. How appropriate.

Lion bought a set for his wife, choosing one that was decorated with unicorns. "Dorothea will love this."

They made several more excursions over the next two days. Town was shy of company even in such a cool summer, but they met a number of acquaintances, including some of the harpies Bear had eluded during the Season. He took great pleasure in telling them he was shopping for presents for his wife.

CHAPTER 26

Bear's letter sounded as if he were following it home, almost on the heels of the mail coach. Rosa half expected to see him the day after Aunt Belle arrived, and hoped he would arrive late in the day after she had a chance to gain answers to some of her questions.

First, though, she needed to visit Father, who Brownlee said had had a bad night. His cough was back, and he seemed more confused than usual, but Brownlee and Rosa agreed there was little point in sending for the doctor. "Even if he agrees to come an hour's drive through pouring rain, he will shake his head and say, 'You cannot turn back the clock,' and we already know that," Rosa said. "I shall order some broth, Brownlee, and perhaps some of cook's lemon and barley tonic."

Downstairs in the kitchen, she found Aunt Belle's maid, Maud, on the same errand. "Madam asked me to give her apologies, Mrs Gavenor. But I knew how it would be. She insisted on making all haste, though we had no reason to flee as if we were chased. We should have stayed put and let That Woman do her worst, but Madam wanted to leave, and she wanted to hurry, and now it has all caught up with her."

So much for Rosa's questions. She told cook to give Maud whatever she needed and assigned Maggie to run any errands Maud might have. Then she wrote a brief note to Aunt Belle, inviting her to stay as long as she wished, and to stay abed as long as she needed.

Bear didn't arrive. Instead, partway through the afternoon, the gig from the inn brought a parcel that had come in the mail. A book, by the shape and size. She opened the note first.

"Dear Rosabel,

I saw three properties yesterday, and one is very suitable for refurbishing and selling, if the owner will agree to an appropriate price. Negotiations may take a few days, so I won't be leaving London as soon as I had hoped.

One of the other properties is of interest, too, and I will tell you more about that when I arrive.

Meanwhile, I saw the enclosed and thought of you. He is, apparently, very fashionable at the moment, or so a lady of my acquaintance told me.

I shall write again, and please keep your letters coming, since I do not know how quickly I will be able to complete my business here.

With affectionate regards,
Gavenor"

Affectionate regards. That was hopeful, was it not? *A lady of my acquaintance* was less so, but she would not allow her mind to drift down that track. Nor would she assume Bear thought she needed to be more fashionable. *Enjoy the gift, Rosa,* she told herself.

The package did, indeed, contain a book, carefully protected between two solid boards, which she removed to see the book itself, small but opulent in tooled green leather, and with gold lettering on the face and spine. "*In My Garden,* by Andrew Delargey." It contained poems; sonnets, mostly. She had not heard of Andrew Delargey, but then, until Bear came, she'd had no contact with the fashionable world.

The pages had been cut, and something slipped between them; a silk bookmark with a long tassel. She pulled it out, using her finger to mark the place, and exclaimed at the pretty thing. It had been skilfully embroidered with roses almost precisely like the rambler that covered the front of Rose Cottage. *How lovely.*

What poem had Bear chosen to mark? She opened the pages and read quickly. *Oh. What could it mean?* It was an ode to a rose, but what a rose! The poet first extolled its beauty, but the poem deteriorated from there as he scratched himself on its thorns and finally found that the lovely colours concealed a black centre, bed to a tiny but venomous snake that struck out at his heart.

Rosa was sitting, the book in her hand, staring at the awful page, when Maud supported Aunt Belle into the room.

Rosa roused herself to help Maud settle the invalid on the couch, with a blanket over her legs and pillows to support her, half sitting. The maid fussed some more, bringing a jug of lemon cordial and a glass, Aunt Belle's spectacles, a book, a package of letters, another rug, "In case of drafts, Mrs Gavenor." She shifted the fire screen, though the fire was not lit, and moved the curtains a little to block a sunbeam.

"Do stop fussing, Maud," Aunt Belle said at last, "and leave me to have a comfortable coze with my niece."

The maid pursed her lips. "Don't you talk overlong, ma'am. You don't want to be back in that bed."

"Yes, yes. Mrs Gavenor shall do most of the talking, and I shall lie here and be comfortable."

Maud grumbled some more, the obvious affection between the two warming their voices.

Finally, she left, shutting the door behind her.

"Now, Rosa, you shall tell me what has you cast in the dumps," Aunt Belle instructed.

Rosa looked at the horrid book, and Bear's note. Perhaps Aunt Belle could explain. "Here. I had a note from Mr Gavenor today." She passed it to Aunt Belle, who donned her little gold rimmed spectacles and scanned it quickly.

"Ah. So you are disappointed that he is delayed?" Aunt Belle narrowed her eyes and examined Rosa's face. "No. Something more."

Rosa passed her the book and the bookmark.

"How pretty!" Aunt Belle said of the bookmark, and, "Andrew Delargey! Why, he is on everyone's lips, or so I am told. A recluse, they say. No one has met him; not even his publisher. Some think the name a *pseudonym*, which means he could be anyone. How very exciting to think one might be at a poetry reading and the man sitting next to one might be the poet himself!"

"The bookmark was in this place," Rosa said, opening the book to the offending poem. Aunt Belle laughed as she read it. "Yes, I heard that Society's favourite poet has recently been disappointed in love, and that his latest book is full of allusions to his false lady. Did you think this intended for you, Rosa? Is your husband the kind of man to send such an insult? I would not have thought from his note he was at all familiar with the poet or his poems. Is he likely to have purchased the book on the recommendation he mentioned and just opened the pages at random to put the bookmark in?"

Rosa nodded thoughtfully. *Yes. Very likely.*

"I think, dear child, that I would like to hear more about this marriage that leaves you so unsure of yourself. Yes, and of your husband, too. I daresay it is his fault; he is a man, after all, but you shall tell Aunt Belle everything and we shall see what might be done."

"I do not know if anything can be done. He married me because the rector said he must, and because he needed a hostess for his business entertainments and a *chatelaine* for his home. Oh, and a child, though how that is to happen when he won't… He said my reputation was of no moment, and that he did not believe what the Pelmans said. Oh, but he does. He does."

Rosa burst into tears and entered the arms her aunt held out to her, finding comfort in the silky, perfumed embrace and the murmured endearments.

She was permitted to indulge for several minutes, then Aunt Belle passed her a handkerchief and commanded her to ring the bell for tea. "Weeping is useful, in its way. But strategizing is better, and for that I need facts, Rosa. Tell me about your reputation. And about the Pelmans, a name I know all too well, to my sorrow."

The meeting with Denthorpe went better than expected. They enjoyed dinner together in a private room at *Fournier's*, and hammered out a deal on the townhouse over the exquisite dishes for which *Fournier's* had become famous. They even managed to sketch broad areas of agreement on the second estate, the one with twenty or twelve houses, depending on whether anything could be salvaged from those left open to vandalism and Mother Nature.

Denthorpe and his agent left, promising to sign in the morning, as soon as the papers they had amended a dozen times in the course of the evening had been copied in a fair hand. Lion and Bear lingered for one more celebratory drink.

"Me for my Dorrie tomorrow, Bear, and you for your Rosa," Lion said.

"I'll drink to that," Bear agreed. His size was a benefit on such evenings. Both Lion and Denthorpe were more than mellow, and Thomas, the agent, had been drinking lemonade for much of the evening.

When they stood to leave, Bear caught Lion's arm to steady him, and they went arm-and-arm through the door of the private dining room and across the floor of the restaurant. Bear paused when he saw Lord Hurley at one of the tables.

"There is someone I wish to talk to," he murmured, more to himself than to Lion, but his friend showed the uncanny ability to shake off the alcohol, a skill that had saved him and his command more than once. A keen glint replaced the sleepy humour in his dark eyes.

"Hurley? I have your back, Bear, but try not to eviscerate him. Fournier's wife wouldn't like it."

They came up on each side of Hurley, each taking a chair from an unoccupied table and seating themselves uninvited. "Hurley," Bear greeted his quarry, ignoring the other three men at the table. "Just the man I wanted to see."

"You bought it sight unseen," Hurley said, his slurred voice indicating he had imbibed even more freely than Bear and Lion. "I told you it was a wreck."

"Not as bad as I feared," Bear reassured him. "I did get one surprise, though. One of the cottages I thought was mine turned out to belong to a Miss Neatham and her father."

Hurley flushed bright red. "Who told you that? Pelman? He promised he would never tell. I suppose he wants it for himself, but I'll tell you this, Gavenor, he already has a wife, so if Rosabel thinks to get his ring on her finger, she'd better watch out."

Bear filed the information away. *A wife, eh? That might reward further investigation.* "You make very free with her Christian name," he observed.

Hurley barked a bitter laugh. "My own half-sister, after all. And my uncle leaving her one of the best properties on the estate. Thankfully, her supposed father was too sick for her to attend the reading of the will, so she never knew."

The disgusting cur. He'd cheated Rosa of her inheritance. But… Hurley's half-sister? The pieces slipped into a new pattern. The Neathams had just the one child, after eleven or twelve years of marriage. He'd ignored the rumours that claimed Rosa was the fallen sister's child, but perhaps they were true. "Your father's daughter by Mrs Neatham's sister Belle." It was not a question.

Hurley's eyes roamed over the other men at the table. "Belle Clifford. My half-sister's mother was Belle Clifford. I ask you! What would you have done if you found part of your inheritance had been left to a woman like that? The base-born brat of Raithby's mistress? She had no right to it."

Bear managed, with some difficulty, to keep his hands from closing around Hurley's neck.

"I was never more shocked," Hurley continued. "I'd even offered her *carte blanche* before I found out. Thank God, she turned me down. I could have bedded my own sister! No, better leave her to Pelman. Turned him down, too, but he said he'd have her in the end."

"Pelman will not be 'having' Rosa," Bear said with laboured patience. "By marriage or in any other way."

Hurley nodded, on and on and on like an automaton. "No need to buy the cow when you get the milk for free," he agreed, at which point Bear's forbearance ran out and his fist connected with Hurley's chin, sending the man's chair tumbling backwards and landing Hurley flat on his back on the floor.

Hurley's three friends surged to their feet, and when Bear turned to look at them, they proved their mettle by sidling out the door. Marcel Fournier, the proprietor, appeared from the kitchen, his brows drawn together in a thunderous frown.

"Please accept my apologies, *Monsieur*," Lion said hastily. "The unconscious gentleman insulted my friend's wife."

"Yes. I am sorry, *Monsieur*," Bear agreed. "Allow us to take out the trash."

Fournier formed his lips into a considering *moue*. "I cannot allow fisticuffs in my restaurant, gentlemen, but nor can any red-blooded man allow an insult to his wife. Remove the *tête de noeud*, and we shall say no more about it."

Bear and Lion carried Hurley outside, where Hurley's three friends broke, alarmed, from a huddled discussion. Lion appointed himself spokesman again. "You may wish to see your friend home, gentlemen. When he is conscious and sober, tell him that Miss Neatham is now Mrs Gavenor, and my friends and I hold her reputation as dear as our own."

"Who is Belle Clifford?" Bear asked, as they sat in Lion's library over one last nightcap. "Rosa's mother, clearly, and sister to Mrs Neatham, but that scoundrel seemed to think we should know the name."

"Raithby's mistress. Not the new Lord Raithby, but the one who has just died. It has been all over the *ton* these past few weeks. His widow threw Mrs Clifford off the Raithby estates, where she has lived for thirty years."

"She was Raithby's mistress for thirty years?" Impressive loyalty in a courtesan.

"According to the new marquess, he told his mother—at the top of his voice and at one of the Duchess of Winshire's afternoon teas, mark you—that *La Clifford* had been a faithful mistress for thirty years, which was more than Lady Raithby could claim as a wife. Unlike Raithby to make any kind of a stir in public, but he always got on better with his father's mistress than his own mother. Even when we were at school."

"You were at school with the new Marquess of Raithby?"

Lion nodded absently. "I've met her, you know. Lady Raithby looks much more the courtesan than Mrs Clifford, who is a dainty wee lady, and must have been very pretty in her day. Beautiful manners, too, and very kind to the schoolboys who came visiting with her lover's heir."

Bear took another sip, absorbing all he had learned. So, Rosa's aunt, really her mother, had not died as Rosa thought, but was still alive, and currently adrift somewhere in the world, having been evicted by her lover's jealous wife. Lion's sympathies were clearly with the mistress and not the marchioness. A dainty wee lady. The villagers all said Rosa took after her aunt. Perhaps he should find Rosa's mother, and make sure she was safe. Safe somewhere far away from her daughter, whose reputation did not need another scandal.

CHAPTER 27

Aunt Belle was not well enough to sit up for long, but insisted upon spending part of each afternoon in the parlour, where she and Rosa exchanged stories and grew to know one another. She was deeply distressed by Rosa's report of the attacks on her reputation. "My fault. All my fault," she mourned.

"Mr Pelman's fault," Rosa retorted. "I have done nothing to deserve his persecution."

"I remember him as an infant, and his sister, too. She was a most unpleasant child." Aunt Belle laughed. "To think, if their father had been sincere in his protestations of marriage, I would have been their stepmother. I had a narrow escape."

She confirmed much of what Rosa had already heard or deduced. At just fifteen, two years younger than her cousin Amanda and five years younger than her sister, she had imagined herself in love with the baron's factor, a charming young widower with two children. He assured her he returned her devotion, and that his public courtship of the squire's daughter was just a show to blind people to his real purpose, since he simply had to see her, and her age made any approach to her uncle impossible.

Belle hugged the secret to herself until the day her uncle

announced a ball to celebrate his daughter's betrothal to Mr Pelman. Shocked, she burst out with what she thought was the truth; that Pelman was marrying her, not Amanda; that they had been meeting in secret; that they loved one another.

Squire Threxton rode for Thorne Hall, where Pelman lived, and was carried home later that day, having suffered an apoplexy. Within days, however, he was well enough to break off the betrothal, and to cast Belle from the house with only the clothes she wore.

"Pelman told him that he had taken what was on offer, which was true enough, but it amounted to a few kisses, and nothing more. My uncle believed the worst, of course. People do. Pelman was waiting for me, but I told him I'd rather starve in a gutter than be his mistress."

"Good for you," Rosa said. Another way in which she and Aunt Belle were alike.

"Matthew, Lord Hurley's nephew, was a captain in the militia and looked very fine in his uniform. I went with him, and if you think your first night with your Bear was a shock, imagine mine! Matthew was kind enough, in his way, but very self-centred."

They talked no more that day, since Aunt Belle was taken by a fit of coughing that left her tired and pale, and Maud and Rosa put her to bed.

The following afternoon, Aunt Belle did not pick up her story, but instead demanded to be told about Bear's courtship of Rosa.

"It was not precisely a courtship," Rosa said. "More a business negotiation."

Aunt Belle, when she had heard the whole story of the proposal, the betrothal, the wedding night, and the aftermath, said, "He blames himself, silly man, and has retreated to lick his wounds."

"He blames himself? For what? I disappointed him."

Aunt Belle laughed. "Rather a lot, poor man. When he comes back, you will forgive him, and welcome him to your bed, and all shall be well, Rosa. Don't expect him to say that he is sorry. Men tend to give presents rather than apologies, I have found. Even Raithby."

The deceased Marquess of Raithby, Rosa had quickly discovered, was Aunt Belle's measure against which all other men were found wanting.

"Bear has been sending me presents, Aunt Belle. Things to help me be the kind of wife he contracted for."

However, Aunt Belle, having read the letters and examined the presents, insisted her view was the correct one. "He is apologizing in his own way, Rosa."

The most recent present was a silver dressing set, with painted ivory inset into the handles, the tray, and the backs of the mirror and brush. "Fairies." Aunt Belle's eyes grew misty. "Raithby used to say I was his good fairy."

"You loved him very much," Rosa stated. *Was he my father?* She had not yet asked whether Aunt Belle was her mother. She could hardly demand to know whether Raithby had sired her, especially since the man who had raised her lay upstairs, miserable with the ague he had not been able to shake off.

"I was his mistress for thirty years. Twenty-eight, in truth, though few would believe it. He rescued me when I was very ill, and asked only my friendship. It was two years before he came to my bed, and then only after his wife had taken up with one of her lovers."

Thirty years, and I am thirty-six. Raithby was not my father, then.

Aunt Belle didn't notice her preoccupation, being absorbed in her memories. "God will take that into account, do you not think? That we were faithful to one another and did as little harm as we could? I am certain Raithby must be in Heaven, waiting for me." She squeezed Rosa's hand, which she was holding. "I think I will rest a little now, my dear girl."

Aunt Belle seldom complained, but Maud confirmed Rosa's fear that she was fading. "My lady was sick before his lordship died, ma'am. But with him gone, she does not want to live, and that's a fact."

"The journey cannot have been good for her."

"Coming to you was good for her, ma'am. She rallied for that. It didn't last, but she will die happy knowing what a sweet lady her sister raised."

CHAPTER 28

At Lion's suggestion, Bear took his questions about Pelman to Wakefield and Wakefield, an enquiry agency with a reputation for knowing everything, or being able to discover it. The principal of the firm proved his worth within minutes, looking thoughtfully at his own ceiling and then announcing, "Interesting. Excuse me one moment, please."

He exited by a door at the back of his office, and returned a few minutes later with a scrapbook, open to a newspaper clipping of an advertisement. The name of the newspaper was neatly written above the clipping, along with the date, March 15th, 1810. Six years ago.

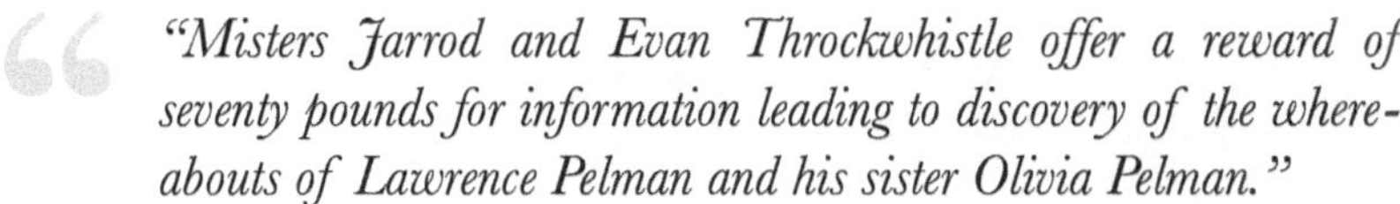

"Misters Jarrod and Evan Throckwhistle offer a reward of seventy pounds for information leading to discovery of the whereabouts of Lawrence Pelman and his sister Olivia Pelman."

Bear let his raised eyebrows ask the obvious question, and Wakefield obliged. "We were asked by a colleague from Glasgow to find out whether the man had come back to London, which Mrs Pelman (sister to the Throckwhistle brothers) understood to be his childhood home."

"Mrs Pelman." Bear tapped the clipping with one finger as he considered that. "He abandoned his wife, then?"

"After divesting her of her dower fund," Wakefield said, adding, with a tight smile, "which makes her brothers most anxious to find him."

"He has spent the last six years in Kettlesworth on the Wirral Peninsula, south of Liverpool."

"His sister, too?" Wakefield took paper from a drawer and wrote down the locations. "I understand Mrs Pelman has a few jewels she wishes to recover from Miss Pelman."

Poisonous pair. Bear hoped the Throckwhistles caught up with them. "Miss Pelman, too."

Wakefield blotted the sheet carefully. "I shall send a message to Glasgow immediately. Thank you, Mr Gavenor."

"One more thing. I'd like you to find someone for me."

When he explained the details, Wakefield refused the commission. "I have already been employed to find Mrs Clifford. The Marquess of Raithby is most anxious to return her to her home in Trenton. The lady is ill, I understand, and Raithby believes himself under an obligation to ensure that his father's dear friend is safe."

"Will you at least let me know if Raithby is successful? I believe the woman to be related to my wife, and I would like to be able to tell Mrs Gavenor that Mrs Clifford is being cared for."

With Wakefield's agreement, Bear was content. More than content. In a few days, he would be home.

Aunt Belle spoke frankly about physical intimacy between men and women, advising Rosa about what to expect, but she refused to discuss what she called harlots' tricks.

"Tricks to deceive one another have no place between lovers, Rosa. That is what you want, is it not? For your husband to love you as you have begun to love him? I know how to weave a spell of sensation into a rope to lead a man by his cock, and I know the limits of that cord. It will snap at the first tug, the first frost." For a moment, she looked unseeing at her cup of willow bark tea, sweetened with honey. Her eyes were bleak. The lines around her eyes spoke of the pain she mostly ignored, or an older pain from the years before Raithby.

"I found that out. Matthew lost interest and passed me to a friend, though I had borne his child and given it up as he demanded."

Me? Rosa wanted to ask. *Was it me?*

Aunt Belle was still talking, "So, I determined to learn all the courtesan arts, and I was sought after, Rosa, do not doubt it. For what good it did me. When I conceived again, and was so ill they thought I was dying, they all deserted me. All but Raithby. He was not one of the men I entertained, but he took me home and had me nursed until I was well again."

"And the baby?" Rosa asked.

"A little boy, Raithby said." She sighed. "He died, poor little mite." She collected herself, took a sip of her tea, and smiled at Rosa, her face calm again. "But we were talking about you and your Bear. For true love, a true bond, you need to be yourself. You need to let him see you as you are."

"It is hopeless, then, because he does not see me. He sees a housekeeper and a hostess, and perhaps someone to help with his business." In his most recent letter, he had praised her decision on the kitchen, so at least she had that value to him.

"I think you underestimate your appeal, but even if you are right, I see in his letters and in what you have told me, a lonely man who needs a loyal friend. Be that friend, and love will grow from friendship."

"His friend?" Rosa frowned.

"Believe me, when a man and a woman are friends—and your letters are taking you in that direction, Rosa—and they also enjoy bed sport, then love is very nearly inevitable. Not, perhaps, everlasting, but your Bear does not appear to be a fickle creature."

"But how are we to enjoy bed sport if you will not help me?"

"I did not say I would not help you, silly girl. I said I would not teach you any tricks."

Despite Aunt Belle telling her that nothing could be done to restore her to health, Rosa sent a message to the doctor, asking him to call when he was next in the vicinity. He came on one of the few fine days the dying summer afforded, reluctantly, tight-lipped.

"Doctor, my aunt is ill. I would like your advice on how we can help her," Rosa said, after performing the introductions.

"Women who sell their bodies seldom die of old age," Dr Whitlow proclaimed, not meeting the eyes of either woman. "I could prescribe mercury, I suppose."

Rosa had her mouth open to throw the man from the house when Aunt Belle laughed. "How flattering that you think me still young enough to have a product to market. I told my niece not to bother you, doctor. I do not believe that mercury is the treatment of choice for lung cancer, which is what Dr Knighton diagnosed when he was good enough to examine me. He warned me I would have perhaps six to nine months before death. That time is up and I am ready to go."

The doctor's eyes widened a little at the name of the respected Society doctor, but he did not soften. "In that case, Mrs Gavenor, I shall take my leave."

In the doorway, he paused. "Laudanum for the pain. There is little else medicine can do in these cases." As if he regretted bending even that much, he brushed past the maid to pick up his hat and hurried through the door as soon as she opened it.

Aunt Belle was distressed. "I must go. The villagers… Rosa, darling, I would not have them shun you for the world."

"Do not worry about the doctor, Aunt Belle. He does not even live in the village. I will not hear of you going anywhere else. You are to stay here where you can be comfortable. The village knows me, never fear."

The village had made up its collective mind. Rosa exchanged a glance with Maud, who undoubtedly had been treated to all the kitchen gossip. Caleb had called Rosa aside to warn her that her aunt was known to be with her, and to be a woman of ill repute. The vicar had lectured her after services on Sunday, telling her that scarlet women should not be allowed to live with decent people, and that her decision to house her aunt told him all he needed to know about her own morals. None of the women who had taken to visiting her in the afternoon had been by in over a week.

However, Aunt Belle did not need to know that, and Rosa was not going to think about what she could not change.

Soon, she had no time to think of anything at all, except Aunt Belle's deteriorating health and her father's cough, which grew worse and worse. When she sent for the doctor, she received a sharp message in return, saying that he would not come. Brownlee called him a useless old fool, and assured Rosa they would do as well without him as with, but Father grew steadily weaker, and so did Aunt Belle.

Rosa spelled first Brownlee and then Maud, catching what sleep she could. The coughing from Father's and Aunt Belle's rooms infiltrated her dreams. She woke tired and dragged her way through each day.

At last, both patients showed signs of improvement. The relentless coughing slowed and almost ceased, and Father—at least—was able to take some broth and keep it down. Aunt Belle still gagged on any food, however soft, so that the best Rosa and Maud could do was keep her mouth moist, but she demanded to be propped up on pillows.

"You and I shall have a nice chat," she told Rosa, "just as soon as I have finished talking to Raithby." The warmth of her smile directed to a point behind Rosa's shoulder had Rosa turning, but no one stood there. Or no one Rosa could see.

"I shall not be long, my love," Aunt Belle assured her delusion, or her vision. "Wait for me."

"You are getting better," Rosa told her, almost begging, but Aunt Belle shook her head.

"I am dying, Rosa. And I am ready, now that I have met you. I saw you once before, you know, when Raithby brought me here for Rosie's funeral. Albert would not let me speak to you, but he sent you into the garden so I could watch you from the window. My dear Rosa. I am so grateful for our time together."

Rosa ignored the tears that insisted on seeping from her eyes. She would miss her chance if she did not ask her question. "Are you my mother?"

Aunt Belle shook her head. "My sister was your mother, and Albert is your father. They raised you and loved you, and you are theirs, never doubt it."

Rosa bit her lip, uncertain how to feel about that answer.

"But I gave birth to you, and Matthew Hurley planted the seed of you in my womb. Is that what you needed to know?"

"Yes." Rosa looked down at the pale, thin hand she held, mottled in blue bruises that appeared without warning, so that both nurses took great care when washing or moving their patient. "Thank you. Thank you for bearing me, and for giving me to your sister."

Aunt Belle looked over to the corner of the room again, lifting her head from the pillows, her voice rising a little with excitement, "Is it time, Raithby?"

The answer must have been 'no,' for she dropped back with a sigh. "I will sleep a little, Rosa. Never doubt that you are loved."

In the morning, Brownlee reported that Father had slept well, which meant Brownlee was available for any service he could perform for Mrs Gavenor. Rosa sent him into the village with a note for the vicar. The man was a fool, but he was ordained to give comfort to the dying. An hour later, Brownlee returned with a blunt refusal. Vicar Snaith would not come to the house.

If only Bear were home. With Father comfortable again, and Aunt Belle sleeping, and both patients watched over by their faithful servants, Rosa took the opportunity to escape to the garden. In her favourite spot, on the seat that overlooked the hens' coop, she re-examined her life in the light of what she now knew.

Lord Hurley was her great uncle. Did he know? She was sure he did, which explained why he was always so kind to her though he could be a harsh man. Crude, too, according to some of the maids, but never to her. Mama was her aunt, and her aunt was her mother. No. Aunt Belle was right; Mama had been mother to her since she was a small baby, and she had not known Aunt Belle at all until these last weeks.

She utterly rejected the idea that Matthew Hurley, Aunt Belle's despoiler, was her father. He had not wanted her, and she did not want him.

How would Bear react when he learned she was base born? She would have to tell him. True love could not be based on lies, Aunt Belle said. *I am greedy. I married Bear for security, and now I want his love.* She would risk her whole future by telling the truth, but what kind of a future would she have, deeply in love with a husband who did not love her back?

She would tell him, and he would be kind, but he would send her away. Bear wanted an heir from his wife, and her blood was tainted for two generations. Aunt Belle said he wouldn't care if he loved her, but he didn't, did he? She was just his convenient wife.

A large tear slid down her cheek and splashed onto her hands, followed by another, and then so many she stopped counting.

"There, there." The voice, and the hand that fell heavily on her shoulder, startled her out of her weeping. She shrank back and looked up into Pelman's face, twisted into a parody of sympathy.

"He has abandoned you, hasn't he?" the loathsome toad gloated. "Forget him, Rosabel. I am still here. I know you want me, and—"

Rosa pushed him, startling him into taking two steps back. Rosa bolted toward the house, but he caught her before she could get by him, grabbed her wrists, and wrapped his arms around her so her hands were trapped behind her back and her body was pressed against his. He bent to kiss her, but she struggled, turning her head from side to side and tucking in her chin so he could not reach her mouth.

She shouted for help, and he spun her around, clutching her body to his with one arm while clapping his other hand across her mouth.

"Let's see what your London whore of a mother has been teaching you," he hissed in her ear as he dragged her farther down the garden, toward the gate that let onto Thorne Hall's park. "Be a good girl, and you might even enjoy it."

CHAPTER 29

A score of miles from Kettlesworth, the carriage full of furnishings and other gifts for Rosa bogged down in mire for perhaps the fifteenth time on the trip from London. Bear and Jeffreys had a well-practiced routine for getting it out, but the broken spoke they found caused a further delay while Bear completed a temporary repair. It would, he hoped, hold until they reached the village blacksmith. If a better repair took longer, he would borrow a horse and ride the few minutes to home. Home, and Rosa.

The wheelwright declared an hour for the task of fixing the wheel well enough for Bear to get his load home. Then the wheel would need to come back for proper repairs, which would take several days. Bear left Jeffreys to bring the carriage home and went to borrow a horse from the inn.

The younger Lady Threxton and her crony, Livia Pelman, waylaid him as he led the horse from the inn yard.

"You have to do something about your wife, Gavenor," Lady Threxton announced with no preamble. "It is a disgrace the way she has been carrying on while you were away."

Stupid jealous crow. Bear attempted to pass her, but the two women moved to block him. "You will excuse me, Lady Threxton. I am in something of a hurry."

"She has her mother staying with her," Miss Pelman said, her eyes avid. "Disgusting, I call it. Flaunting the woman in the face of the village after all she has done."

Oh no. Not Belle Clifford. Rosa, what were you thinking? Bear did his best to pour oil on gossip's turbulent waters. "Her mother is dead."

Too late. The chorus of harpies continued, first one of the pair, then the other, certain of their ground.

"Not the woman who claimed her. Her real mother. The London harlot. We don't allow that kind of thing in this village."

"The vicar has told her that the woman must go, but she will not listen to him."

"Yes, and your wife has not been to services for three weeks. That just tells you."

"What about that Liverpool man who works for you? Very friendly with your wife, he is." *Stupid cow. You could not have picked a more unlikely person. Caleb Redding is devoted to the wife who waits for him in Liverpool.*

"That is enough," Bear roared, so that they both shrunk back, and he shouldered his way between them, heedless of manners. "You will not abuse my wife in my hearing." *Petulant, nasty women.* Even if Rosa had been foolish enough to take in her sick mother— and she would. He'd never met a woman more heedless of her reputation. Even so, he refused to believe she had a disloyal bone in her body. Not his Rosa.

He pressed the horse into a gallop. He'd soon see what was going on.

The horse was fresh and made short work of the hill, and in minutes, Bear approached the gate of Rose Cottage. He pulled the horse to a halt. Better calm himself before he went inside. In his current frame of mind, all his protective instincts aroused by the village scandal-mongers, he was likely to lose his temper and say the wrong thing. He dismounted and took several deep breaths, his eyes on the gate.

What was Pelman doing here? Leaving, apparently, opening the gate and coming through, then looking around and flinching when he saw Bear. He hid the flinch by straightening and puffing out his chest, pushing his shoulders back. "Home are you, Gavenor? About time, but you'll have to wait in line. I've had my turn, and now Redding is having his. They're around the back in the garden."

Bear returned sneer for sneer and shoved the poisonous weasel out of his way. "I'll deal with you later," he promised. Was Rosa in the garden? Only one way to find out. He rounded the house, scanning what he could see. No Rosa.

He was about to enter by the back door when a puff of breeze brought the sound of murmuring voices. There. Shadows in the shrubbery near the gate to the park. One shadow, rather. A small woman in the arms of a tall man.

Several of his soundless strides brought Bear close enough to confirm what his eyes reported, despite the denial of his mind and the screaming desolation of his heart. Another two steps and he ripped Caleb away from Rosa, felling him with one murderous punch.

His anger roared in his ears, painted his wife's face with a red haze. Someone called her a filthy harlot. Was that him? His throat was raw with shouting. He wanted to hit Caleb again, but the man was unconscious.

Rosa was shouting back, but he couldn't hear her words, couldn't let them in while the anger raged. Someone had bruised her neck, scratched her face. Her dress was torn, too. She'd been crying. The eyes glaring at him were red-rimmed. She wagged a finger at him, and suddenly Bear knew he had made another mistake.

He backed away, then broke and ran, brushing past the servants who were hurrying to Rosa's support.

CHAPTER 30

Bear ran around the house, and in moments Rosa heard a horse galloping away. Mrs Gillywether enfolded her in a hug, and Sukie bent to Caleb, who opened one eye and then the other, and looked the way Bear had gone before pushing himself up. "Gone, has he? Stupid Duffer. Never you mind, Mrs Gavenor. I'll explain to him when he gets back."

If he comes back, Rosa thought. She sent Caleb with the cook, to get a steak to put on his eye, and asked Sukie to bring her warm water to wash in while she changed out of the torn dress.

By the time she settled herself in Belle's room, she was feeling more hopeful. His reaction suggested his feelings for her were strong, and surely the word he had been babbling before he fled—after the horrid insults she refused to remember—was 'sorry.'

Belle was unconscious, and her breathing irregular—two or three shallow breaths followed by a long pause that had Maud and Rosa sitting forward, waiting for the next. Death could not be far away.

Maggie came to fetch her when Jeffreys arrived with Bear's carriage. Jeffreys was astounded to hear that Bear had left again.

"He was that keen to be home, Mrs Gavenor. If he told me once, he told me a thousand times."

Rosa was not going to gossip about her husband, though the other servants would tell Jeffreys what happened. "I expect he will return soon," she said.

The carriage was full of extravagances. A little writing desk and chair, several paintings of roses, jewelled dancing slippers, packets of comfits, two more bonnets—each more expensive than anything Rosa had ever owned.

She let Jeffreys bring all the gifts in and lay them out around the parlour, then took the smallest of them up to Belle's bedroom and sent Maud off to have her evening meal.

Alone with the aunt who was also her mother, Rosa displayed the gifts, described what had happened in the garden, and explained her conflicting feelings. Though Belle did not respond, still Rosa felt she knew what Belle would say if she could. "He will come," she said aloud. "He would not have reacted so violently if he did not care about me, and when he has had time to think, he will come home."

However, when she went to say goodnight to her Father, and ordered the doors shut against the night, Bear had still not returned.

Rosa was determined to stay awake, feeling somehow that Belle would continue to live as long as Rosa watched. However, Rosa woke with a start in the first light of dawn to find Belle dead, her relaxed face looking years younger, her lips curved in a smile that seemed a promise of joy.

Maud, when summoned, burst into tears and proclaimed that Madam was happy now, and with His Grace, and Rosa could not argue with the maid's theology.

Bear examined the tankard from which he had been drinking. He'd slept properly for the first time since leaving his poor wife crying in the garden, and thus was nearly sober again. He could finish the tankard and go inside the scruffy hedge tavern to demand another, or he could go home and pay for his sins. Neither option appealed.

He looked up as a shadow fell across his table. "So, there you are, Mr Gavenor."

"Jeffreys?" What was his manservant doing here?

"Two days, I've been looking for you." Jeffreys shook his head slowly. Even watching the motion sent Bear's head and stomach into rebellion. "Ever since you run off from poor Mrs Gavenor, leaving her in such trouble."

"Rosa is in trouble?" That brought him to his feet, though he groaned as the full weight of his headache hit him.

Jeffreys leant a supporting hand to Bear's elbow. "Need to get you cleaned up so you can go home and help her."

"Redding can help her," grumbled Bear.

Jeffreys cast his eyes upward and sighed. "That's just nonsense, and you know it. He's telling people he got his black eye when he rescued Mrs Gavenor from that swine Pelman, but Pelman is saying you gave it to him. And if you did, then you should be ashamed, sir. Pelman, too, for assaulting the poor lady with her father sick and the poor London lady on her deathbed."

"Mrs Clifford is dying? Hell and damnation, Jeffreys. I have been an ass."

Jeffreys kept his face bland. "Yes, sir. I wouldn't presume to argue with you, sir."

Bear shook off the supporting hand and led the way into the disreputable place he'd come across in his flight. "Less of the lip, Jeffreys, and tell me exactly how big a hole I've dug for myself, and what trouble my lady wife faces. Do it while you help me get presentable. If I am going to crawl home seeking forgiveness, the sooner the better."

"The sooner the better indeed, sir. The lady died. Mrs Clifford. The vicar is refusing to give her a funeral or space in consecrated ground. Mrs Gavenor won't go anywhere without two guards from the work site because of that Pelman."

Bear issued a string of hearty curses, and Jeffreys nodded agreement before going in search of the landlord and a bucket of hot water.

Soon, Bear was retracing his steps toward Rose Cottage, mounted on one of his own horses, Jeffreys following and leading the hired horse. Within half an hour, they reached Thorne Hall's rear gate and Bear turned in. "We'll take the shortcut, Jeffreys, and I'll stop to apologize to Caleb on my way."

Caleb was found overseeing a gang of workers who were taking advantage of the fine day to seat the main beam of the new stable block.

Bear pulled his horse up beside his foreman, who watched him with wary eyes. "I've come to apologize, Caleb. I was completely out of line."

The man raised one eyebrow. "You were. But you should be apologizing to your wife."

Bear accepted his employee's censure meekly. "I know. I plan to. I plan to keep doing so till she gives me another chance, though I don't deserve it. I don't seem to think clearly when that woman is around."

The foreman lifted one corner of his mouth in a wry smile, but his tone was sympathetic. "Love does that to you."

The word hit Bear like a mallet. *Love.* Love had not been part of the bargain, but there he was, in up to his neck. Deeper, having treated his wife so badly she might never forgive him. After all, what had he done to show his love? Hurt her, deserted her, abused her.

"You rescued her from Pelman, I take it." He hoped.

"Just in time," Caleb confirmed. "Have you been to the house?"

Bear looked toward the bridle track. In a few minutes, he would see her. "Not yet. I stopped here on the way."

"Better go," Caleb advised. "And Mr Gavenor? From one married man to another, tell her that you love her. Women need to hear the words."

The vultures had gathered—the vicar, the squire and his wife, the Pelmans, a group of the more conservative and judgmental villagers. All had come to bolster the vicar in his determination to stand outside the gate and lecture Rosa on her evil ways and her certain damnation.

Bear observed from the shadows of the trees. Rosa faced her accusers with a dignity that touched his heart. "You are offensive, sir," she told the vicar. "You have listened to the calumnies of false witnesses."

"Your own husband bears witness by his absence," said the vicar, triumphantly.

That was Bear's cue. He stepped into view, leaving Jeffreys to manage the horses. "Mrs Gavenor's husband bears witness by his presence." As he spoke, he covered the ground in long strides and plunged straight into the group, which scattered to avoid him. "Dear wife, I apologize for the delay in my arrival. How may I be of service? Shall I remove the litter from outside our gate? Do these people not realize this is a house of mourning?"

He reached Rosa and bent to greet her with a kiss on the lips, ignoring the startled look she gave him before she returned it. He had some grovelling to do, but he wouldn't undermine her position by doing so in public. Turning back to face the crowd, he said, "Vicar, if you are not here to make arrangements for the funeral of my aunt by marriage, then you are not welcome."

Lady Threxton pushed her way to the vicar's side. "You know your duty, Mr Snaith."

Bear ignored him while glaring at Pelman, who was whispering urgently to his sister at the side of the crowd. "Pelman, I hear you have continued to persecute my wife. I warn you now, your past is on its way to catch up with you. Count yourself lucky that I am too busy to give you the thrashing you richly deserve, and get yourself home, lest I make time to remedy the lack."

He gave Lady Threxton's indignant protest one contemptuous look and turned to the squire. "Threxton. You and your household have been helping this snake and his vicious sister to spread lying rumours. You know best why. I suggest you take your wife home and meditate on whether your own lives would stand up to the scrutiny of my investigators. I assure you, Mrs Gavenor's reputation would not suffer from such an examination, and Pelman's are now known to me and are about to catch up with him."

Bear turned and put one arm around Rosa. "Let us go inside, dearest. We have much to talk about."

He looked back over his shoulder. "Vicar Snaith, my next errand shall be to see the rector about your stewardship of his parish. I am not impressed, and I don't believe he will be."

Snaith sputtered, still looking after the Pelmans, who had hurried back to their buggy and were already on the road back to the village. Sir Gerard bit his upper lip as he watched the pair. "What do you mean, Gavenor? If you know something to Pelman's discredit, spit it out."

"I have just arrived home, Threxton. If the mystery does not solve itself in a day or two, I'll make a point of calling on you." While Bear and Sir Gerard spoke, the villagers had been deserting the crowd, fading backwards or sideways and strolling off as if they had merely paused from curiosity while out on an afternoon walk. When Sir Gerard took his protesting wife's hand, placed it firmly on his arm and escorted her to his gig, the vicar found himself abandoned.

"I suppose you had better come inside," Bear said without enthusiasm. If Rosa wanted a respectable Christian burial for Mrs Clifford, then Bear would do whatever it took to make him cooperate.

"Show Mr Snaith into the parlour," he instructed Maggie, who stood at the front door gawping. "My wife and I will be with you shortly," he told Snaith before whisking Rosa into the study. She came, unresisting. A good sign, he hoped.

Inside the study, with the door closed, she withdrew her elbow from his cupping hand, her face set in worried furrows. She was pale, with bruises under her eyes that indicated lost sleep, and she was nearly as thin as the day they met. "You have not been eating properly," he said.

That did the trick. Up went her chin, and her lips set before she counter attacked. "Mr Gavenor, I…"

She had every right to heap recriminations on his head, but he couldn't bear to hear her call him 'Mr.' as if they had not become friends through their letters. As she paused for a breath, he broke in, "I deserve you should be so formal. I wasn't here when you needed me. I jumped to assumptions when I did come home."

"Mr Redding was not…"

"I know. I knew almost immediately." She had not stepped away from him, and the anxious lines were smoothing. He took advantage of her proximity by capturing one small hand in both of his. "I know that I owe you a grovelling apology, and you shall have it, but first I want to tell you I will support whatever you want. For your aunt. Tell the vicar your requirements for the funeral and I will make sure it happens."

"Mr Ga—"

He raised her hand to press a kiss on it and she blushed.

"Hugh… You don't understand. I don't deserve…"

He unfurled her fingers and pressed another kiss into her palm. "You deserve every good thing, and have been left to carry your burdens alone for too long. Let me help, Rosa. It is my duty and my delight. Come. We cannot leave Mr Snaith alone much longer or he will take to his heels."

The vicar insisted that Mrs Clifford had died a sinner. "If she did," Bear pointed out, "then so did the Marquess of Raithby, and he was buried with full honours from St Georges."

"If she did," Rosa added, "you must accept part of the blame, since you refused to bring spiritual comfort to my aunt when I sent for you."

They negotiated a plot near Rosie Neatham's, in the far corner of the churchyard, and a funeral service two mornings hence, at an unfashionable time of day, which Snaith clearly thought might save him from the village's censure.

At last, Rosa and Bear were alone. *Now is the time for that grovelling apology.* Before Bear could find the right words, Rosa spoke. "Hugh,

I need to tell you…" her voice trailed off. Bear was not the only one struggling to put feelings into words. Perhaps they should leave this discussion until tomorrow, until she had caught up on some sleep.

He put out a gentle finger to trace the blue marks under her eyes. "You need to rest. When did you last have a solid night's sleep?"

Rosa stamped her foot. Hugh suppressed a grin. She would not appreciate it, his little thorny fairy.

"Hugh, you must listen to me." A defiant lift of her chin, which looked eminently kissable. "It is true. What the villagers said? About my aunt really being my mother? It is true. So, you see, I am not a fit woman to be your wife." So that was the maggot in her head. Moisture gathered in the corners of her eyes before she veiled them with her lashes, looking down at the hand he had recaptured. "I am sorry, Hugh. Are divorces very expensive?"

"Very. Do you want a divorce?" He pulled her a little closer so he could kiss her brow. "I know I have been an abysmal husband, but I promise I will do better. I have been taking lessons from a married friend. I forgot them for a moment the other day. But I remember now."

Rosa lifted her face to give him access to her eyes and her cheeks. "You are not paying attention. I am the daughter of a fallen woman. I have been living a lie all my life. Aunt Belle sent me to her sister and her husband to raise as their own."

"Yes. That is what I guessed. Does it upset you, Rosa? It doesn't worry me. According to my friend Lion, your mother did the best she could with the circumstances in which she found herself. Your aunt, I should say. Your Aunt Belle may have birthed you, but the Neathams were your mother and father."

Rosa evaded his lips to ask, "Do you not mind? That a notorious courtesan gave birth to me?"

Bear, encouraged by her lack of resistance to his advances, cupped her face in his large hands and looked deep into her eyes. "I don't know what drove her to that life. I do know that you are kind, and good, and gentle, and that I am not fit to clean your shoes. But I am lucky enough to have you for my wife, and I shall spend a lifetime making sure you feel lucky, too." He lowered his lips, and this time she rose on her toes to meet him.

CHAPTER 31

Sometime later, Rosa, now seated on Bear's lap and considerably flushed and rumpled, said, "Pelman."

"He won't bother you again."

"Not him," Rosa said. "His father. Pelman senior drove my aunt to that life, when he courted her in secret and then became betrothed to her cousin."

"Like father, like son! Don't tell me Pelman senior was your father." The previous baron had thought Rosa his great niece, but only Mrs Clifford would know for certain.

Rosa drew away from him, wrinkling her nose as if at a foul odour. "No! No, that is a disgusting thought. Surely, he would draw the line at seducing a possible sister? The current Lord Hurley did, in any case, when he came to hear the will read. He avoided me, and left almost immediately, so I suppose my Lord Hurley let out the secret in his will, and Aunt Belle confirmed it. Matthew Hurley, my baron's nephew, ran off with my aunt after Pelman ruined her."

"The will left Rose Cottage to you and your father. Yes, and a lump sum to invest. Hurley told me. He and Pelman conspired to cheat you, but I have the deed to the cottage. Not the lump sum, I'm sorry. Hurley is in the suds." The idiot, addicted to gambling, had lost everything, including the price Bear had paid for Thorne Hall. A distraint on his remaining property would fetch them very little, but at least Rosa's name on the deed for Rose Cottage had kept it from being lost with the rest.

"Rose Cottage is ours?" This time, Rosa initiated the kiss, and by the time it ended, Bear had her bare to the waist.

"We had better stop now, my dear wife. I do not mean to press for your favours until you are ready."

"I am no longer wincing when I sit," Rosa pointed out. "Will you come up to bed with me, Hugh? I so want to find out the 'more.'"

Puzzled, Bear repeated, "The more?"

"When we—you know—when we did *that*, before the pain and even after it, a bit, I was certain there was something more." Rosa blushed scarlet as she spoke, and her state of undress showed that the blush reached down her neck to her lovely breasts. Which, if Bear was wise, he would ignore in favour of listening to what his wife was saying. "Something I was reaching for. Aunt Belle said I was lucky to feel that way so soon. She said there is more, and you could show it to me." She began to slip her arms back into her sleeves, and Bear managed to drag his eyes from her nipples.

"Promise you will talk to me," Bear said. "Tell me how you feel—what you like and what you don't like."

Rosa smiled. "I will if you will. Promise you won't go away if either of us fails. Stay and talk to me, Bear, instead of retreating into yourself." She frowned down at her bodice, which was now missing several buttons.

Bear picked up a shawl that was draped over the sofa and wrapped it around Rosa so the deficiency in buttons was hidden from any watching servants. "I will if you will," he told her. Then he picked her up and carried her up the stairs to their bedroom.

The next day, Bear took Rosa into the village to finalize the arrangements for the funeral. Rosa kept darting glances at Bear from under her eyelashes, her cheeks heating as she recalled the activities of the night. And the early morning. Aunt Belle had refused to describe the 'more' she was reaching after, and she had been right, Rosa decided. It was beyond explanation, and Bear had earned the smug expression that settled on his face when Rosa told him that.

They stopped outside the inn, and left Jeffreys to care for the horse while they walked to the rectory. At the corner, they waited for the passing of a smart traveling carriage, dusty now with travel but still gleaming with gilt and polish through the dust.

They reached the other side of the road when the carriage pulled up, and a man as elegant as his equipage leapt down without waiting for his servants to lower the steps.

"Mr and Mrs Gavenor?" he called, and they stopped to wait for him.

The man bowed, a shallow inclination of his head and upper body. "How fortuitous that you are visiting the village at this moment. I was coming to see you."

Bear returned the bow with the same depth of courtesy. "Have we met, sir?"

The man waved the remark off. "No, no. But Lion described you as a sort of blond mountain, and—of course—I would have known Mrs Gavenor anywhere. You are the exact image of Aunt Belle, Mrs Gavenor. I see you, and I am ten again, being invited to take another biscuit. She always kept biscuits to treat us when we rode over."

Ah. Now Rosa knew who he was. "Lord Raithby, I assume." Aunt Belle's stories about the affection between her and the marquess's children were true then.

"My wits have gone begging!" Raithby exclaimed. "Yes, I am Raithby, though I cannot say I am accustomed to it yet. Aunt Belle? Did she come to you? Is she well?"

"I am sorry," Rosa said. "She died just two days ago."

Raithby's eager smile faded. "I am too late, then. But she came to you? She died happy?"

"She died fully confident that she would be reunited with your father," Rosa said.

"And she saw her niece before she died." Raithby smiled. "That would have pleased her. She sometimes spoke of you, Mrs Gavenor. She wanted very much to meet you, if she could do so without her position causing you harm."

"We are on our way to the rectory to arrange her funeral, Raithby," Bear said. "As an interested party, would you care to join us? We could do with your social position to persuade our reluctant minister of Mrs Clifford's respectability."

Raithby bowed again. "I am at your service."

Bear began walking again, his hand covering Rosa's where it rested on his arm.

"You must wonder at my wishing to be here." Raithby strolled on Rosa's other side. "The fact is she made my father happy. She was also kind to a group of neglected children and encouraged him to spend time with us. It was thanks to your aunt that I grew up knowing the love of a father. I will always be grateful to her for that."

"My mother," Rosa said, with a sideways glance at Bear to see if he objected to this disclosure. He merely grinned and gave her hand a light squeeze.

"I always suspected, and she confirmed it when I gave her your letter."

"I have only just discovered it."

"We are almost brother and sister, Mrs Gavenor. Rosa, I should say, because Bear is brother-in-arms to one of my dearest friends, and you are my sister not-quite-in-law."

Bear pressed Rosa's hand closer into his side, but made no comment. They were at the rectory gate, and shelved further discussion until after the interview with Vicar Snaith.

I t was a quiet funeral. Rosa had bowed to custom and stayed at home, after making Bear promise to tell her all about it. Bear thought he and Raithby would be the only mourners, but Sir Gerard Threxton, wearing a black armband, arrived as the service was starting. He lingered to speak to Bear after the interment. "My condolences to your wife, Gavenor." He turned his hat in his hands, looking down at it as if for inspiration. "Mine and Lady Threxton's, that is."

"Good man," Raithby said encouragingly, and Threxton shot him a grateful look. "Well, yes. Cousins, you know. As Lord Raithby said when he called yesterday, families should stick together." *A mystery solved.* Bear decided he should be grateful for Raithby's interference, rather than irritated that he, rather than Bear, had given Rosa peace with her remaining family.

"M' mother… She is living in the past, Gavenor. You understand. But my wife sees the sense of dropping the feud."

"Nothing to feud about," Raithby said.

Bear felt Rosa was owed more for a lifetime of estrangement and two years of persecution than to have the past swept under the mat. "I will ask my wife if she is willing to accept your apologies, Sir Gerard. Perhaps you and Lady Threxton might call tomorrow afternoon?"

Threxton's nostrils flared, but he glanced again at Raithby and then nodded. "That is fair. What might have happened to Mrs Gavenor if you had not come…" He shuddered. "I was never more shocked than when Pelman's brothers-in-law laid their case before me so I could order the scoundrel's arrest. Miss Pelman, too. My wife is horrified she put her trust in such a woman."

Jeffreys had heard about the dramatic arrest and passed the news on to Bear during his morning ablutions. The Throckwhistle brothers and their men had carried both Pelmans off to Glasgow, where they would certainly need to face the wronged Mrs Pelman and might have to answer to charges of theft and fraud.

Threxton spun his hat one more time, then clamped it onto his head. "Tomorrow, then. Good day, Gavenor, Raithby. Raithby, I dare say… That is, my wife asked me to invite you to dinner."

Raithby inclined his head slightly. "Please thank Lady Threxton for me, but tell her that I am beginning my journey home almost immediately, as soon as I have taken my leave of Mrs Gavenor."

With that, Threxton had to be content.

As they walked to Rose Cottage, Bear wondered out loud how long the cease fire would last, once Raithby was gone.

Raithby smiled, his eyes full of mischief. "Longer than you might think. I made it clear that Aunt Belle was a treasured member of our family and that so, by extension, was her niece. Oh, and I may have hinted that your wife and I were correspondents. The younger Lady Threxton is quite awed to think she is cousin by marriage to a lady who exchanges letters with a marquess. I figured the blasted title might as well be of some use."

The marquess had one more surprise for them, saying as he prepared to leave, "Rosa, Aunt Belle's house belonged to her free and clear, and my mother had no right to dispossess her, as I have made clear to my solicitors and my servants."

"I think she did not care, Raithby," Rosa assured him. "She took it as an excuse to come home, and I am glad she did."

"Beyond a doubt. But now the house is yours. It belongs to you as her nearest relative, and I will send you the deeds."

"Set it up as a dower property, Raithby," Bear advised. "I have my lawyers doing so with Rose Cottage, to give my Rosa security should anything happen to me."

Raithby nodded approval. "A good idea. And Rosa, if ever this mountain you have chosen treats you poorly, come to me and I will look after you."

That was almost the final word except for goodbyes and good wishes. Raithby's traveling carriage and his servants waited at the gate, and soon Rosa and Bear stood on the doorstep watching the marquess and his entourage out of sight down the lane.

"Good," Bear said. "He is gone."

"I thought he was nice," Rosa objected.

"I thought him too damned familiar with my wife."

"Are you jealous, Hugh?" Rosa sounded delighted.

"Yes, dammit. I am jealous, though you never give me cause."

Bear lifted his wife to bring her head closer to his own, his hands supporting her delightful behind. "I am jealous of every person you smile at, everything that captures your attention. I find that love makes me selfish, my dearest—an old bear guarding its honey. Do you mind?"

Rosa put a hand on either side of his face and carefully examined him. "Love, Hugh?"

"Love," Bear affirmed. "I love you, Rosa. I didn't bargain for that, but I hope you will learn to love me, too."

Rosa brushed her lips over his. "I do, Hugh. I fell in love with you long ago, the first time you went out in the rain for the sake of an impudent intruder and rose thief. I love you more and more with every passing day."

Bear shifted his head back so he could see her eyes. "How very convenient our marriage is turning out to be," he observed, then settled his mouth over hers, and they lost themselves in a kiss that ended only when Maggie whipped open the front door, saw them, and slammed it shut again.

"We are scandalizing the servants, Hugh," Rosa said. "Perhaps we should find somewhere more private?"

Bear hoisted her more securely in his arms, and nudged open the door so he could carry her up to bed. A wife he loved, one willing to enjoy bed sport in the day time. He had not had either of those on his list when he went shopping for a bride. "Very convenient," he repeated.

THE END

REGENCY BOOKS BY JUDE KNIGHT

LION'S ZOO

New series about officers from an elite cadre of exploring officers returning to England and find love and danger.

Chaos Come Again

Tormented by his past and by vile rumours, will this Regency Othello allow a liar he trusts to destroy the love between himself and his wife?

Grasp the Thorn (This book)

An accident brought Rosa and Bear together. Secrets, self-doubt, and malicious rumours may tear them apart. Can they grasp the thorn of scandal to gather the rose of love?

One Hour in Freedom

Matt (Bull Moriarty) and Electra ran in the same street gang as children, and were lovers as young adults. Now he is an officer in the Thames River Police, and she has been sent to kill him.

PUBLICATION IN NOVEMBER

The Darkness Within

Max enters a religious community to find a former comrade. The peace he finds almost seduces him. But the secrets the community hides are even darker than Max's own.

PUBLICATION IN DECEMBER

A TWIST UPON A REGENCY TALE

Fairy tales (loosely) reinterpreted as Regency romances, but with magical elements transformed into natural happenings and the role of hero and heroine reversed.

Lady Beast's Bridegroom (Book 1 in *A Twist Upon a Regency Tale*)

Is the love of Beauty and his Lady Beast strong enough to overcome prejudice, hatred, and rejection?

The Talons of a Lyon (Part of the Lyon's Den Connected World)

Lance promised Mrs Dove Lyon he would take Lady Frogmore from Pond Street into High Society. Her nasty relatives are determined he will fail.

PUBLISHED APRIL 2023

One Perfect Dance (Book 2 in *A Twist Upon a Regency Tale*)

For sixteen years, Ash has owed Regina a dance. His stepbrothers will do anything to keep him from the ball.

PUBLISHED MAY 2023

Snowy and the Seven Doves (Book 3 in *A Twist Upon a Regency Tale*)

The hero raised in a brothel. The heroine born to wealth and title. The villain who wants to destroy the first and own the second.

PUBLISHED AUGUST 2023

Crossing the Lyon (a novella in Night of Lyons)

The golden tickets are a trap for two innocent maidens. But who will the trap catch?

PUBLISHED AUGUST 2023

Perchance to Dream (Book 4 in A Twist Upon a Regency Tale)

Scared by life, they have abandoned dreams of romance. Until love's kiss awakens them.

PUBLISHED SEPTEMBER 2023

THE GOLDEN REDEPENNINGS SERIES

True love is rare and elusive, but they won't settle for less

Candle's Christmas Chair (A novella in *The Golden Redepennings* series)

They are separated by social standing and malicious lies. He has until Christmas to convince her to give their love another chance.

Gingerbread Bride (A novella in *The Golden Redepennings* series)

Mary runs from an unwanted marriage and finds adventure, danger and her girlhood hero, coming once more to her rescue.

Farewell to Kindness (Book 1 in *The Golden Redepennings* series)

Love is not always convenient. Anne and Rede have different goals, but when their enemies join forces, so must they.

A Raging Madness (Book 2 in *The Golden Redepennings* series)
Their marriage is a fiction. Their enemies are all too real. Uncovering the truth will need all the trust Ella and Alex can find.

The Realm of Silence (Book 3 in *The Golden Redepennings* series)
Rescue her daughter, destroy her dragons, defeat his demons, return to his lonely life. How hard can it be?

Unkept Promises (Book 4 in *The Golden Redepennings* series)
Mia hopes to negotiate a comfortable marriage. Jules wants his wife to return to England, where she belongs. Love confounds them both.

The Flavour of Our Deeds (Book 5 in The Golden Redepenning series)
When Luke finally admits to loving Kitty, she thinks their troubles are over. They are just beginning.
PUBLISHED IN MARCH 2023

The Golden Redepennings: Books 1 to 4
THE FIRST FOUR BOOKS OF THE SERIES ARE NOW AVAILABLE IN BOX SET FORM:

THE RETURN OF THE MOUNTAIN KING

In 1812, high Society is rocked when the heir to the Duke of Winshire, long thought dead, returns to England with the children of his Persian-born wife and fierce armed retainers.

To Wed a Proper Lady: The Bluestocking and the Barbarian (Book 1 in The Return of the Mountain King series)

Everyone knows James needs a bride with impeccable blood lines. He needs Sophia's love more.

To Mend the Broken-Hearted: The Healer and the Hermit (Book 2 in The Return of the Mountain King series)

A woman doctor from a foreign land and a recluse earl with a missing hand find common ground nursing the children he loves, whether they are his or not.

Melting Matilda (A novella in the Return of the Mountain King series)

Sparks flew a year ago when the Granite Earl kissed the Ice Princess. In the depths of another winter, fire still smoulders under the frost between them.

To Claim the Long-Lost Lover: The Diamond and the Doctor (Book 3 in The Return of the Mountain King series)

The beauty known as the Winderfield Diamond hides a ruinous secret. Society's newest viscount holds the key.

To Tame the Wild Rake: The Saint and the Sinner (Book 4 in The Return of the Mountain King series)

The whole world knows Aldridge is a wicked sinner. The ton has labelled Charlotte a saint for her virtue and good works. Appearances can be deceptive.

Paradise Triptych (A collection in The Return of the Mountain King series)

Long ago, when they were young, James and Eleanor were deeply in love. But their families tore them apart and they went on to marry other people. This set of two novellas and a set of memoirs tells their story.

OTHER NOVELS

A Baron for Becky

She was a fallen woman. How could the men who loved her help set her back on her feet?

Revealed in Mist

As spy and enquiry agent, Prue and David worked to uncover secrets, while hiding a few of their own.

House of Thorns

His rose thief bride comes with a scandal that threatens to tear them apart.

OTHER NOVELLAS

The Husband Gamble [This novella]

When the pawn becomes Queen, she and the opposing King will both win the game of love.

Lord Calne's Christmas Ruby

One wealthy merchant's heiress with an aversion to fortune hunters. One an impoverished earl with a twisted hand. Combine and stir with one villainous rector.

A Suitable Husband

A chef from the slums, however talented, is no fit mate for the cousin of a duke, however distant. But Cedrica can dream.

The Beast Next Door (A novella in the Bluestocking Belles collection *Valentines from Bath)*

In all the assemblies and parties, no-one Charis met could ever match the beast next door.

A Dream Come True (A novella in the Bluestocking Belles collection Storm & Shelter)

The tempest that batters Barnaby Somerville's village is the latest but not the least of his challenges. He does not expect the storm that will batter his heart.

Lord Cuckoo Comes Home (A novella in the Bluestocking Belles collection *Desperate Daughters)*

Two people who have never fitted in just might be a perfect fit.

LUNCH-LENGTH READS: STORY COLLECTIONS

Hand-Turned Tales and Lost in the Tale

A double handful of short stories and novellas, free from most eretailers. Try the range of Jude's imagination one bite at a time, in a lunch-length read.

If Mistletoe Could Tell Tales

A repackaging of six published Christmas stories: four novellas and two novelettes. Because nothing enhances the magic of Christmas like the magic of love.

Hearts in the Land of Ferns

Five stories all set in New Zealand: two historical and three contemporary suspense. All That Glisters has been published in Hand-Turned Tales. The other four have all been published in multi-author collections, but never before in a collection of Jude Knight stories.

Chasing the Tale and Chasing the Tale: Volume 11

Short stories just long enough for a lunch or coffee break. In volume 1: Nine Regency plus one colonial New Zealand and one medieval Scotland. In volume 2: mostly Regency, with one Victorian New Zealand. Multiple tropes, catastrophes and barriers on the way to a happy ending.

AUTHOR NOTES

THE YEAR WITHOUT A SUMMER

In 1816, after an unusually severe winter, the United Kingdom experienced 'a summer more unseasonable than any former one in my remembrance' (from correspondence between Susan Farington and Antony Hamond). Nurseryman Samuel Curtis called it 'the most unpropitious season ever remembered', and diariest Pegge Burnell called August 'a most unseasonable month', describing it elsewhere as 'dismal, wet, and cold'.

Various studies in the United States, England, and Europe have concluded that this was more than regular climate fluctuation, although winters in the last decade of the eighteenth and early part of the century had been exceptionally cold. Sunspot numbers were down; volcanic activity was up. And then, in 1815, Mount Tambora in Indonesia erupted in the largest volcanic eruption in, perhaps, thousands of years. For hundreds of miles, the sea was covered in pumice. Ash darkened the sky so that candles were needed throughout the day, and even with candles, people could see only a few metres. Tens, and perhaps hundreds, of thousands of people died. And high in the atmosphere, tonnes of sulfur dioxide thrown out of the volcano turned in sulfuric acid, making an aerosol that would block incoming solar radiation for years to come.

It took time for the effects to reach the other side of the world, but the record shows that the spring, summer, and autumn of 1816 were exceptionally wet and cold, with frequent storms and floods. Harvest failed in the United States, Britain, and across Europe and

Asia, leading to famine on a wide scale and starvation among the poor. In China, peasants turned to growing opium in order to make money, and the boom in production led in time to the Opium Wars and the opium trade that still exists today.

In England, people were already suffering severe hardship and food shortages because of the long years of war, harsh economic policies that favoured the wealthy, and the vast mass of unemployed swollen by more than 400,000 men from dismissed from the army and navy after the war. Adding a volcanically enhanced winter to the mix was devastating.

> *...despite the long run of generally cold wet conditions experienced in the 1810s, extreme weather recorded in the spring, summer and autumn months of 1816 may have been 'truly exceptional' and 'of a degree for which it is reasonable to invoke an external forcing mechanism' (Sadler and Grattan 1999, 187).*

FERRIES TO THE WIRRAL PENINSULA

people have been running a ferry service across the Mersey for well over a thousand years. Historians agree that such a service, by row or sail boat, predates the Benedictine Priory at Birkenhead, but once the monks were established, they did their best to monopolise the trade. Annoying for the other locals, but useful for historians, since we have the records of the court cases they took to try to stop other providers.

The monks charged for the service, which helped to pay for the hospitality they offered travellers at the abbey. Some of the unauthorised providers were less scrupulous, overloading their boats and charging much higher fees.

After the dissolution of the monasteries, the right to offer a ferry service changed hands a number of times, and at tunes several formal services were offered, as well as the age old recourse of the traveller: a request to any inhabitant with a boat: 'I'll give you a bob if you row me over the river'. Travellers were advised to set the price before they got into the boat, and not to pay till they got out.

At the time I'm writing about, there were at least five routes operating: Liverpool to Woodside (the original route that the monks established), Liverpool to Seacombe, Liverpool to Eastham, Liverpool to Tranmere, and Liverpool to Rock Ferry.

The first steamship operated between Liverpool and Runcorn in 1815. The Elizabeth was a wooden paddle steamer, measuring 58 feet and 9 inches in length, and with a cabin that could take around a hundred passengers. The cousins behind the service were two teenagers, one a naval officer and the other a member of the local militia. It cannot have had the reception they hoped for, because the ship was sold in 1816 and the company dissolved.

In 1816, the steam packet Greenock replaced the Elizabeth. The Greenock was 85.3 feet in length. She remained less than a month on the Runcorn run, before being transferred to the Liverpool to Ellesmere Port route, taking travellers to and from the Chester canal.

Other steamers also criss-crossed the River Mersey in 1816, and soon more followed. The ferries were no longer dependent on the wind, and could run to timetable, which made the service much more reliable.

And the crossing was quick. The time recorded for the Aetna, which began a service from Liverpool to Tranmere in 1817 and continued for fifteen years, is five minutes.

TWENTY-FOUR YEARS AN OFFICER

I thought you might appreciate a very brief overview of Bear's army career.

My character Bear Gavenor joined the army when he was sixteen. Since he is forty-two in 1816, the time of the book, he might have served in India, the West Indies, or Ireland. Cavalry being expensive to transport, they tended not to be sent to as many away games as the rest of the army, so he probably spent part of his time on duty in England. He was a captain by the time he served with Lion in the Peninsular campaign, and he sold his commission after Napoleon's first surrender.

While he talks about being two years out of the army, he volunteered for Waterloo in 1815, arriving early in June and leaving again five weeks later after Napoleon surrendered for a second time.

I'm figuring he probably started his investment in houses that needed renovation during the Peninsular campaign, travelling back to England while the army was in winter quarters and setting Caleb up as his project manager. Their relationship obviously goes back a bit, and by 1816, he is making serious money.

PROPERTY DEVELOPERS IN THE GEORGIAN AND REGENCY ERA

Most English cities, and particularly London, grew significantly in the eighteenth and nineteenth centuries.

Wealthy families who owned land in and around large cities, especially London, were the Georgian era's property developers. Great landowners developed well planned streets and squares on the western side of London, obtaining local acts of Parliament to allow them to levy rates so they could finance paving, lighting, cleaning, and watchmen.

The standard of construction was generally high, and many—from grand aristocratic residences to more modest workers terraced houses—still remain today, giving many cities and towns their character.

Lesser developers built with cheap materials and little planning, and left slums and neglect. These dwellings are almost all gone.

Most buildings were designed by owners and builders together—until the middle of the eighteenth century an architect was anyone who cared to call themselves one.

I haven't found a specific example of a Regency man making his fortune by flipping houses. But why not? In a world where fortunes were being made and lost, renovating houses for the upwardly mobile seems like a good thing to do. If people like Bear didn't exist, it was necessary to create one. So I did.